THE FIRST ADVENTURE OF SIR ERROL HYDE

Book One Of A Trilogy

Book Two
The Second Adventure Of Sir Errol Hyde:
The Case Of The Oxford Rasputin

Book Three
The Final Adventure Of Sir Errol Hyde:
The Case Of Wittgenstein's Secret Notebook

THE FIRST ADVENTURE OF SIR ERROL HYDE

THE CASE OF THE WAYWARD PRINCE

Gay Hendricks

Printed in the United States of America

First Printing, 2017

ISBN-13: 978-1-945949-35-7

Waterfront Digital Press
2055 Oxford Ave
Cardiff, CA 92007

https://waterfront.zendesk.com/hc/en-us
http://www.waterside.com/

CHAPTER ONE

I departed the comforts of my flat and set off down Sloane Street on my morning's mission. It was ten o'clock on a chilly Saturday, a time when I'd normally be savoring breakfast with an attractive sleepover guest. Instead, I was pitting myself against the blusters of a windy London day. I didn't mind, though; I had literally the noblest of reasons.

A courier had brought a royal summons early that morning, beckoning me to Buckingham Palace, there to consult with a prince of the realm. The Palace offered to send a carriage for me but I insisted on walking. I was very much in need of some fresh air to cleanse my stuffy head, the after-effects of last night's smoky evening with a young woman of theatrical ambitions, one of those modern women who must show the world how sophisticated they are by puffing on the new miniature tubes of tobacco they call "cigarettes." However, one must sometimes make sacrifices in life, because those same smoke-tinged lips, so offensive to the tongue, could also wolf one's nether appendage with heartfelt gusto (the quality I find most essential for a practitioner to bring to the task.)

Thirty minutes later I was aired out and brimming with zest as I strode through one of the side entrances of the Palace and presented myself at the prince's apartments. After a short wait I was ushered into the regal presence; the prince was seated at a table, surrounded by a gaggle of assistants. He made a hissing sound and his minions scattered from the room.

"I say, Roller, it's been far too long," the prince said, using the college-era nickname I detested even then.

To show him I couldn't be bullied, I lobbed his own freshman moniker back at him, "Yes, it has, Possum, too long indeed." I believe I saw him wince slightly when the word "Possum" hit his ears. In actual fact, we could barely stand each other at Cambridge and our relations hadn't improved a great deal over the years. I considered him to be a witless drudge who took ordinariness to levels one seldom sees, even among members of the royal family. Had it not been for the good fortune of being one of old Victoria's countless offspring, he would have probably had a long and uneventful career as an office drone buried deep in the bowels of an insurance firm.

I cut to the point. "What can I do for Your Royal Highness?"

He made his characteristic harrumph and said, "Put simply, we find ourselves butt-up in a muddy scrum."

The prince fancied himself a "regular guy," one of those fellows who like to regard life as a sporting event. I, by contrast, do everything possible to avoid "regular guys." As for sports, except for billiards and golf you can shove the lot of them. As my Grandmother Hyde so wisely said, "A gentleman should not play any sport that's likely to evoke a grunt."

I couldn't help needling the old Possum a little. "When you say '*WE* find ourselves butt-up' are you perhaps referring to *YOU*, the royal personage himself?"

Harrumph. "I'm afraid so," he said.

"And how exactly would you like me to help?"

"Damn it, Roller, you've always been good at the whole 'thinking' sort of thing. It's never quite been my strong suit. I could use some of your counsel."

Indeed. The prince had scraped through Cambridge only with the assistance of a team of tutors that did everything but carry him to his exams on a palanquin.

"Your Highness has other exemplary qualities," I ventured, although I could not at the moment bring to mind exactly what they were.

"Just so," he said.

"And what is it you need this fabled 'thinking' of mine for? Give me the details of the scrum and I'll see if I can dream something up."

We were interrupted at that moment by a female child who came bounding into the room, accompanied by a small, yapping dog. The two screeched to a halt next to me and craned their necks up to inspect me. For some reason I've never quite understood, children and animals love me extravagantly, even though to my knowledge I have never given the slightest indication that I welcome their affections.

The prince said, "Sir Errol, meet my daughter, Princess Margaret, known to all as Maggie. Maggie, bid welcome to my old friend, Sir Errol Hyde."

"Welcome to you, Sir Errol," the girl sang out, her voice a veritable clarion bell of brightness and cheer. "And this is Arthur!" she chirped, pointing at the little dog, which was bouncing vertically up to my thigh approximately every 1.5 seconds, three yaps to the leap.

"Yes," the prince said, with some distaste, "That's Arthur."

I should mention that the prince's own given name was Arthur, making one wonder which member of the family had bestowed the tiny yapper's moniker on him.

"Papa, be nice to Arthur," the girl said, pulling a sad face.

The prince gave the youngster's head a friendly tousle. "Of course, dear. Now run along and play, Maggie. I must conduct important business with Sir Errol."

"Yes, Papa," the girl said, dashing off with Arthur trotting behind.

The prince leaned over and whispered in a conspiratorial tone, "Unlike myself, my wife is quite a passionate enthusiast of all things canine. I find their constant yelping and toadying to be somewhat exasperating."

"Well," I suggested, naively as it turned out, "You are, after all, the prince, husband and head of household. Couldn't you place some sort of royal ban on the irritating critters?"

The prince gave me a weary smile. "You're not married, are you, Sir Errol?"

I admitted that I had not yet abandoned myself to the joyous gavotte of matrimony.

"Then I will not attempt to explain," he said, his face an Old Master portrait of noble sacrifice. "I prefer the company of a cat, and although her Highness cannot abide them, she does allow me to maintain the companionship of old Clyde here in my offices." He gestured toward a couch, on which reposed a vast, fluffy cat I hadn't noticed.

"I confess absolute ignorance of all such creatures," I said. "Sadly, my childhood was bereft of pets, save for a succession of parakeets kept by one of my step-mothers."

The prince said, "I find Clyde to be an indispensable ally in maintaining my sanity as I go about my princely duties. The old fellow appears to have absolutely no consideration for my elevated station in life. He will stroll over my lap casually, try it out for comfort, and then walk right off if he doesn't find it suitable. His attitude is most refreshing, given the amount of bowing and scraping I must put up with every day."

I was quite certain the prince had not invited me to discuss the relative merits of household pets, so I did a little clearing of my own throat to urge His Highness to get to the point.

He harrumphed back at me and said, "Yes, let me elucidate a few more details."

"Please," I said.

"Well, bluntly put, we have been shagging a new chambermaid in the household's employ and it has led to certain complications."

With a tiny tickle of glee playing around my innards I pressed him again: "And when you say 'we,' do I presume you mean it is *you* who have been doing the aforementioned shagging?"

He nodded, making a glum face. "Roller, I'm in it up to the pantaloons. You've got to help me extricate myself."

In spite of the 'Roller' references I found myself warming to the task. I fancy myself something of a specialist in affairs of the heart, and there's hardly anything I like better than an extrication of this sort. My understanding of the inner workings of the female mind is especially prodigious.

I asked him point-blank, "Has your dalliance, perchance, accidentally resulted in the gestation of a royal bastard?"

"Good God, no," he said, with a massive harrumph. "Even I know not to insert myself into that particular aperture."

He pointed to his mouth with one hand and patted his bottom with the other. "The young lady cheerfully receives the royal member in places that my wife does not see fit to use for congress of a carnal nature."

My mind tried to picture the Princess, with her famous ramrod straight posture and her perpetual expression of sniffing an unpleasant odor, giving an enthusiastic toot to the princely appendage. The effort caused a slight twinge of headache in my left temple.

"Then what precisely is our complication, Your Highness?"

He unburdened himself of a long, heavy sigh. "The young lady is Bulgarian," he said.

"Certainly regrettable as a matter of principle, but I don't see how her Bulgarian identity plays into our particular dilemma."

Harrumph. "Apparently Bulgarians have very strong family bonds, and this particular Bulgarian comes attached to two brothers who are both very large and very protective."

"Ah, so. And have these burly brethren paid Your Highness a visit?"

"Heavens, no. However, they accosted my butler after church last Sunday and gave him a rude thrashing. They said it was to send me a message."

"My word!" I said. "You've been without a butler all week?"

"It's been a terrible inconvenience," he said, "but a footman stepped up and has been covering for him tolerably well."

"How is the poor fellow doing?"

The prince said, "Not badly, considering his lack of proper training."

"I meant the butler."

"Oh yes, of course. I'm happy to say he took the beating in a manly way. He's a sturdy Yorkshire lad and you know how they are. Not a chirp of complaint out of him."

"I'm sure he saw the greater good."

"Quite," the prince said. "To ameliorate his suffering we are considering upping his salary by two shillings a week, enough for him to buy an extra pint or two down at his local pub."

"More than generous," I said. "Now, pray tell, what do these bellicose brethren appear to want?"

He thrust a battered piece of paper into my hand. I peered at it and saw a few sentences scrawled in pencil.

YOU HAVE BROUGHT SHAME ON OUR FAMILY. YOU MUST PAY. COME TO THE HOUND AND CUDGEL IN WHITECHAPEL AT 5 PM TUESDAY TO TALK TERMS.

"It's wretched impertinence, is what it is," the prince said. "How dare they suggest that a member of the royal family meet them in a pub! And in Whitechapel no less!"

It had been years since Jack The Ripper wreaked his mayhem upon the prostitutes of Whitechapel, but the name of that slum-infested suburb still was not spoken in polite company.

I made a murmur of sympathy.

"Thank God my mother is no longer alive!" the prince said. "She would have gotten wind of this in an instant and had my scalp."

Old Victoria had been in the ground a couple of years, but her considerable presence still hovered over the land. During her long reign she had gained a formidable reputation for knowing every speck of gossip that slipped the lips of Palace servants.

I said, "Yes, your sainted mother, may she rest in peace, would have been all over this situation like cognac on Christmas pudding.

Best to keep it deeply under wraps. To that point, Possum, how many people know about this dilemma?"

"The butler, of course, and my personal secretary, Kudlow. That's all." The prince cast a sideways look at me. "I thought about consulting Holmes."

Oh my, the prince has a wily side, I thought. He's trying to set the hook by pitting me against my cross-town rival, Sherlock Holmes.

"No doubt Holmes would do a first-rate job," I offered cheerily. "I would recommend him with only the most minor of reservations."

His Highness cocked the royal head to one side. "You are far too enthusiastic to be sincere. I've heard that you and Holmes are not the best of friends. What's your beef about, anyway?"

"No real beef. Of course, he is jealous of my knighthood, but on a deeper level, Holmes has little resonance with affairs of the heart." I continued with my friendly critique of Holmes. "If Your Highness would permit an observation common among the spatherdabs who spend their days passing gossip about, Holmes has been living with a gentleman friend far too long to be completely free of suspicion."

"Dear God!" the prince exclaimed. "We're not talking buggery here, are we?"

I pretended not to hear and sailed right along. "The only other problem with Holmes is his alarming tendency to permit his cases to be written about in pulp magazines."

The prince nodded vigorously. "I had come to the same conclusion, Roller. That's why I summoned you first. So far your exploits have not been immortalized in print. I wish above all for this to be handled quietly."

"Nothing Holmes does is ever done quietly," I said. "The man goes after publicity like an anteater on the snuff."

"Quite," said the prince. "Now, man to man, can you help me?"

"Of course," I said. "Consider the matter over and done with."

The royal orbs flew wide open. "Really? And how much do you figure it will cost? I'm on a bit of an allowance, as you no doubt know."

I certainly did know; the cost of maintaining the royal family had been a subject of great debate in the press. The boys of Fleet Street had even been so crass as to publish the allowances of all Queen Victoria's royal offspring. It amounted to hundreds of thousands of pounds a year, so I did not feel overly concerned that the prince was just scraping by.

"You won't pay them a farthing," I said, causing relief and a gleeful grin to break out on the princely countenance.

"If you can do that, dear boy, you're the magician everyone says you are. I was prepared to spend a hundred pounds sterling to get these beefy Balkans off my back."

I batted my eyes to give the appearance of modesty.

The prince rang a bell and in popped his secretary, Kudlow, a worried-looking little fellow with pince-nez glasses.

"Kudlow, bring me a purse," the prince said. Kudlow dashed off and returned a moment later with a plush, purple purse. The prince shook out a dozen or so gold sovereigns onto the table; the coins made a satisfying series of solid clinks.

"Surely you'll need some expense money, the cost of carriages and such," the prince said, scooping up the gold and offering it to me.

I pocketed the gold with barely a murmur of dissent. Truth be told, a bit of extra gold would come in handy, because later in the day I was taking delivery of a new pair of boots the good gnomes at John Lobb had been laboring over for the past few months. The boots would cost me about five of those sovereigns, leaving me with plenty to put in the palms of people whose assistance I required along the way.

In spite of what my colleague over on Baker Street might say, money is one of the best friends a detective can have. I've tried to read a few of Dr. Watson's accounts, and one false note in the stories is that

Holmes never seems to bribe anyone! I made a mental note to needle him on that subject next time we crossed paths on the social circuit.

I noticed the prince fingering a gold sovereign from the purse, a dark look on his face. He held the coin aloft, indicating the noble profile of his eldest brother stamped on the coin, King Edward VII.

"Why does he get to have all the fun AND be the king, too?" the prince asked, with more than a trace of irritation. The king was notorious for his many affairs, carried out with the tacit approval of the Queen. "He gets to frolic with every desirable woman in the kingdom, from Lilly Langtry to Lady Churchill. Me? I have it off with one chambermaid and get my butler thrashed! Where's the fairness in that, Roller?"

"Your Highness indeed bears a heavy burden," I said. "However, I will attempt with my efforts to lighten it somewhat." I promised the prince I would report back within 24 hours about the progress I had made. I gave him reasonable assurance the matter would be settled by then.

"Before I go, I should like to have a word or two with the young lady under discussion."

"Kudlow," the prince said, "Please fetch her."

Kudlow scurried out of the room.

The prince said, "I think you will have a deeper understanding and perhaps more sympathy for my plight when you meet her."

"What is the young lady's name?"

"Ariana."

"And the last name?"

"Utterly unpronounceable. The English tongue is not capable of such gymnastics."

In a few moments Kudlow opened the door and ushered in to the room a woman so gorgeous and sensual that all I could do was stare at her with my jaw agape. She was of medium height, but that was the only medium thing about her. She had jet-black hair tucked up under her cap and a bosom one could get lost in, plus a generous bottom with scenic contours even her plain skirt couldn't conceal. Her almond-shaped face, glowing skin and long eyelashes gave an appearance of youthful freshness combined with worldly beauty. I became aware of a guttural sound behind me and realized it was a low groan escaping the prince's mouth. He was clearly transfixed and I could see why. It was only through great restraint that I was able to withhold a groan of my own.

I exchanged a few pleasantries with the young lady, which she entertained with eyes discreetly lowered, speaking in an unusual accent a-slither with sibilants. I listened keenly to get the correct pronunciation of her last name. After a few bits of polite conversation I said my goodbyes and beat a hasty retreat. The prince's guttural utterances were becoming more audible and I did not wish to be an impediment to his amorous pursuits.

There was work to do, but I was quite certain I already had the case solved.

CHAPTER TWO

"How is the fit, sir?" asked Cyril, my boot-man from the John Lobb shop. He had been kind enough to bring the just-finished boots around to the flat for me to try on.

"Perfectly comfortable," I said, getting a radiant beam of pride out of Cyril. Cyril had been the boot-maker for my father and grandfather as well; he remarked that both my departed ancestors would be proud of me for carrying on the family tradition of being shod by Lobb, the King's own cobbler.

Based on my own observation, I had my doubts that either of the old boys had ever felt any detectable human emotion. I kept that opinion to myself, not wanting to tamper with the rosy glow on Cyril's face. "No doubt," I said. "And the Hyde family is most grateful for your fine craftsmanship." Cyril writhed with pleasure.

Clad snugly against the brisk wind and wearing my gleaming pair of new boots, I set off to my barber for a shave and quick trim before applying myself to my detective pursuits. When I got up to the corner at Pont Street I peered through the window of T. Jeffers, Gentlemen's Barber, to see if I could grab a chair. Seeing that both chairs were unoccupied, I stepped inside and plopped myself on one.

"Good Day, Sir Errol," Timothy called from the back of the shop.

"And to you, Timothy."

He darted up and bundled me in the traditional cape. He wrapped a warm towel around my face and laid me back in the chair.

"Sir Errol," Timothy said, lifting my locks and running his fingers through them, "You have the hairline of a man half your age."

He leaned in and asked, with a conspiratorial chuckle, "Are other parts of your constitution also functioning with the robustness of a twenty-year-old?"

I'd long indulged Timothy in taking liberties with me regarding the subjects he was prone to discuss. In particular, Timothy was obsessed with the sexual habits of the upper classes. He regarded members of the privileged class to be a separate species, one that the commoner must study with the care of an anthropologist. He had cut my hair since I was a lad, and counted on me to give him the unadorned perspective on the matter.

I assured him all my parts were in fine working order.

"How is Lady Forsythia?" Timothy asked.

"Fine, fine," I murmured from inside the warm confines of the towel. "Her charitable works are proceeding apace. She's busy as usual elevating the plight of various groups who need elevating, urchins and such."

"Lady Forsythia is an icon of compassion," Timothy intoned piously.

I grunted my assent.

"But does the dear lady still resist the full, radiant expression of your passion, Sir Errol?"

Cheeky bugger. He just had to press that sore spot, didn't he? Once, in a moment of regrettable honesty after a particularly good haircut, I'd revealed to Timothy that the one area of thwarted intention in my otherwise perfect existence was that Lady Forsythia steadfastly clung to her no-sex-before-marriage policy.

"She has her reasons, Timothy. Let's give her that."

"Indeed, sir, and I'm quite certain those reasons are solid as mahogany. But has the lady ever explained what those reasons are, Sir Errol?"

"It was something along the lines of 'Errol, we in the upper classes must strive to behave impeccably, so we may serve as an example to those less fortunate than ourselves. How can I counsel a young female urchin to save herself for marriage when I'm shagging it off on the side with my boyfriend?' "

Timothy gasped, but like a dedicated anthropologist recovered enough to say, "Forgive the possible impertinence of my question, Sir Errol, but did Lady Forsythia actually use the phrase, 'shagging it off'?"

"Yes, Lady Forsythia frequently expresses herself in terms that might be considered salty."

Timothy for once was stunned into silence as he tried to digest this shocking piece of information. He peeled off the towel, lathered my face up generously and began scraping away my whiskers. Afterwards he gave me a light trim around the ears, anointed me with various oils and lotions and pronounced me fit to walk the streets of the metropolis.

As he was helping me on with my coat Timothy recovered enough to sympathize a bit more with my plight. "Sir Errol, one would think your elevation to knighthood might have caused a loosening of Lady Forsythia's principled stand."

"No, sadly, she was not moved to relax her standards, God love her. She's been surrounded all her life with dukes, duchesses and all manner of royalty, so a mere knighthood would hardly impress her."

He couldn't let it go. He said, "Still, one would think she might throw the new knight a bone, as it were."

"Steady on, Timothy." Sometimes you have to remind a fellow of his place.

"Quite so, Sir Errol. Sometimes my inquisitive mind gets the better of me." He gave my coat a final dust-off and ushered me to the door.

I tipped him more lavishly than he deserved and headed out to hail a carriage. The driver gave me a wary look when I told him I wanted to go to Whitechapel, but a few shillings in his palm relieved his anxieties.

It had been a while since I'd put my feet on the filthy streets of Whitechapel, and as soon as I did I began to regret wearing my new boots. I had to prance nimbly from one step to the next to avoid stepping in some foul pile of detritus. But if the streets were awful, strewn with trash and reeking of manure, they were nothing compared to the inhabitants of that miserable quarter. As far as the eye could see in that teeming cauldron of so-called humanity I beheld the lame, halt and blind competing for begging space with wall-to-wall urchins. By the time I got to The Hound And Cudgel I was grateful I remembered to bring a cologne-scented handkerchief to hold to my nose.

I pushed my way through a huddle of drunks lounging near the front door and entered the tavern. The interior of the pub was even grubbier than the streets outside. I was grateful for the acrid cloud of cigar smoke, noxious to the nose though it was; it helped cover up the revolting smells wafting from the armpits and other unwashed regions of the clientele. Peering through the dim interior I could make out at least a dozen inebriants lurching about, making a din of noise that assaulted my ears worse than the time Lady Forsythia dragged me to a Wagner opera.

I stood in a corner near the door, figuring that the Balkan Brothers would soon discern my identity. I stood out from the crowd somewhat, not only due to my Savile Row suit and gleaming new boots, but also because I wore the only face in the place unblemished by soot and grime.

Presently a serving-wench sidled over and leered up at me, exposing a mouthful of teeth that resembled a moonlit graveyard in Wales. "Does the gentleman fancy a drink?" She gave me a lurid wink. "Or perhaps a bit of entertainment for his afternoon pleasure?"

I politely declined the offer of "entertainment" and ordered a pint of bitter to while away the time. I didn't have to wait long. Hardly had I swallowed my first swig of beer before two beefy fellows separated themselves from the multitude and lumbered over in my direction. They both wore big overcoats and knit caps pulled down over their ears.

One of them had a drooping moustache and the other a full, black beard; their bent and lumpy noses told me they were no strangers to a brawl. The bearded one sized me up and down and said, "You ain't the prince."

"Hardly," I said. "Princes don't come in places like this. I am here to represent His Highness."

"Aw right, then, do some representing," said Moustache. "You got our message. What's Hizzonor gonna to do to make this right?"

"Absolutely nothing," I said.

Beard snarled and stuck his belligerent chin out. "That ain't gonna work, buster. You seen what we done to that butler fellow."

I corrected him. "I haven't personally seen the butler but I understand you gave him a rude thrashing."

"That ain't nothing like we're gonna do to you if you ain't handin' over some money for our sister."

"I have a better idea," I said. "Would you like to hear it?"

That brought them up short. "What sort of idea?" Moustache asked.

"First, let me make some friends," I said. I went over to the bar and put a gold sovereign on the counter. The bartender's eyes almost popped out; he probably hadn't seen a coin of that magnitude in his establishment's history.

"Hello, my good fellow. Will this buy a round for the house?"

He looked around the room, no doubt doing a head count. "It'll buy a shot of whiskey and a pint of bitter for 'em, and you'll have a few shillings coming back at you."

"The change is all yours, my good man, plus a tad more." I laid out ten shillings on the counter beside the gold sovereign. The bartender looked at me with such gratitude that I feared for a moment he might lunge over the bar and wrap his tattooed arms around me.

"Well, then, you got yourself a deal. Shall I commence to pour?"

"Would you please announce it to them in terms they'll understand?"

"Sure thing, governor." He reared back his head and bellowed, 'THIS FINE GENTLEMAN IS BUYING A PINT AND A DRAM FOR THE HOUSE. LET'S GIVE THE GENT A HAND!"

A might roar burst from their throats as they clapped wildly; the thirsty hoard surged to the bar to collect their *lagniappe.* When I stepped back over to the two Bulgarian brothers I found them staring at me with mouths wide open, precisely the effect I wanted to achieve. Previous experience had shown me that people from the Balkan regions have an immense capacity for astonishment.

Now that I had the crowd on my side, in case of any unpleasantness from the Bulgarian contingent, I felt safe in making my proposition.

"The prince was prepared to give you each a gold sovereign, but I am here to make you an offer, anyway."

"We're listening," Beard said.

"Let's go outside so I can breathe," I said.

They reluctantly agreed and we exited the tavern, pushing ourselves through the jumble of drunks loitering near the door. Blessedly, the sun had broken through the clouds and was bathing the street in a radiant glow equal to a splendid summer day. I was pleased; I needed good light.

We found a spot on the sidewalk out of the way from passersby. I extracted a piece of paper from my pocket and held it aloft. "I want to propose a marvelous new deal, boys. I would like to offer you one gold sovereign each now and this piece of paper to sign. Once you have signed it I will give you too more."

Beard snarled and shook his head. Moustache, however, had a better head on his shoulders than his brother. He said, "What's on the paper?"

"Well, take a look." I handed him the paper.

Beard broke in with, "We can't read English, you idiot."

I paused momentarily to consider the nerve of someone who couldn't read English calling me an "idiot." However, I decided to ponder that issue on an occasion when I didn't have thirty stone of Bulgarians in front of me. I couldn't help asking, though, "Why don't you learn? It would be immensely helpful in expanding your services."

"We don't like it," Beard said.

I'd never heard of anyone disliking an entire language. "But why? Exactly why don't you like it?"

Moustache said, "You got too many words for things. You don't need all them words. Where we come from rain is rain. You don't need all them other words like drizzle and sprinkle."

I surrendered in my vain attempt to improve their lot. "All right, I'll read you what the paper says." I took the paper back from him and opened my mouth to read it.

He stopped me with a grunt. "Ain't no need. Just give us them coins and we'll sign it. You ain't never gonna see us again anyhow."

"I would feel better if I read it to you, anyway."

They shrugged and looked bored while I rattled off the words to them.

"We, the undersigned, hereby demand money from you. If we don't get paid we guarantee we will do bodily harm to you and your friends. If you give us money we will keep our mouths shut about you and Ariana Keskkulla. We also swear and certify that the aforementioned Ariana Keskkulla is not Bulgarian or our sister."

Oddly enough, the only thing they asked me about was the last point.

"How did you know she weren't our sister?" Moustache asked.

I said, "None of your business," and indicated the place for them to sign. "That's your business right there. All you have to do now is sign and you will be able to hold these in your own hands." I opened my palm and revealed a handful gold sovereigns. Their eyes bulged.

I offered them a pen and watched them scrawl their names on the paper.

I inspected their signatures. "Ivan Dragusha is it? And Viko Dragusha?"

They bobbed their heads, their eyes riveted on the sovereigns.

"Excellent. Now hold out your hands and enjoy the pleasure of feeling gold sovereigns drop into them just for putting your name on a piece of paper."

They stretched out their hands and as I dropped the coins I turned to the left and produced my most rugged, heroic smile. The flash went off, capturing the moment for all time.

A voice behind them said, "You boys are under arrest."

Inspector Dinwoodie, my man from Scotland Yard, stepped forward, flanked by two burly Bobbies brandishing their night-sticks. The Brothers Dragusha went into a slump and surrendered themselves to the handcuffs without a peep. They'd obviously been through the drill before.

The inspector removed the gold sovereigns from the brothers' clutch and gave them back to me. I pressed them back into his hand.

"Please keep them for the Widows and Orphans fund, Inspector." I plunked another one into his palm. "And here's one to buy a round for the boys down at The Badge And Whistle."

He clasped my hand, touched nearly to tears.

I thanked him and hastened to go.

"The thanks go to you, Sir Errol, for taking these two miscreants off the streets."

"You're too kind," I said. "I'll drop by the precinct this week for a cup of tea with the fellows."

"I know they'd appreciate it, Sir Errol."

I turned to Leo, the photographer, who was just packing up his case. I gave him a half-crown and asked when he could drop the print by my flat.

"On your doorstep tomorrow by noon," he said. "Thanks for the work once again, Sir Errol."

"The pleasure is mine, Leo."

I had, of course, asked the carriage to wait while I carried out my business. I waved to the driver, who was parked across the street. He made a U-turn and pulled the carriage up beside me. I got in and settled myself on the seat, but before we could pull off there came a knock at the window. I looked out to see a lean, tall, heavily bearded fellow standing next to the carriage, attempting to get my attention. From his rumpled clothing I deduced him to be a beggar of some kind. I slid open the window and asked him what he wanted.

"Why the photographer?" he asked, rather bluntly I thought.

"What business is it of yours?" I asked, putting a bit of flint in my tone.

"All London is my business," he said, giving me a sly grin.

Suddenly it dawned on me. "Good God," I said, "Is that you, Holmes?"

Indeed it was, disguised behind a phony Old Testament beard and dressed in the shabbiest of clothing. He gave me a slight bow and a tiny smile.

"What on earth are you doing in Whitechapel wearing that get-up?" I asked.

"I have gone undercover to work a case, but I observed your little performance and couldn't help wondering what purpose the photographer served."

"Simple," I said. "I'm writing a book about my adventures."

"Really! A book for grownups?"

"Certainly."

"Why would a book for grownups have pictures?"

"It's an up-and-coming idea in the literary world."

"I don't believe I've heard of such a thing," he said.

"I'm sure you haven't, but then, you don't do much of your own writing, do you?"

He gave me the famous Sherlock Holmes hard stare, the tiny pinpoints of his pupils glinting like obsidian. All it did was make me wonder about what substances he had been imbibing. There was talk he had become overly fond of the new wonder drug, cocaine, recommended by the notorious Viennese doctor, Sigmund Freud.

I had tried cocaine myself once when it first became fashionable, but all it did was make me careen around the room having rapid-fire conversations with fascinating people who, as soon as the drug wore off, returned to being just as boring as they were before I had partaken. Any drug that makes upper-class English people seem fascinating is far too dangerous to trifle with. Let us simply pray it doesn't fall into the hands of the lower classes! If they start thinking *they're* fascinating—even for brief periods of time—it could wreak havoc on the delicately balanced social structure we maintain.

As far as cocaine is concerned, Sherlock's welcome to the lot of it. When I imbibe I like to be taken in the direction of ease and merriment, rather than into the manic state cocaine induces. My body is sensitive to all but modest amounts of alcohol, so a half-pint of ale or a glass of Bordeaux gives me all the ease I need. However, for the heights of merriment I require I often complement my modest alcohol intake with the excellent hashish I came to enjoy during my sojourns in Lebanon and the Kulu Valley of India. The herb had always served me admirably, both by adding a touch of mirth to life's daily round and by warming the passions of lady friends in whose companionship I was luxuriating.

Holmes said, "So far, Dr. Watson seems to be doing a decent job. I'm told the recent issue of the Strand magazine sold out in a matter of days."

I could feel heat building in me along with an urge to reach out and punch his aquiline nose, an effect Holmes always seemed to produce in me if I'm around him for more than a minute or two.

"I must go," I said.

"Certainly," he said. "You no doubt need to report back to the member of the royal family on whose errand you are engaged."

That gave me a jolt, I don't mind saying. But he wouldn't leave it there.

He said, "You also need to clean those new boots you just got from the John Lobb emporium before you go to call on Lady Forsythia."

By God, the cheek of the man! I fixed him with my most baleful glare and said, "Have you been following me, Holmes?"

He threw his head back and laughed. "Of course not, Sir Errol. It was the simplest of deductions. I observed that your boots shine as boots only do when recently purchased, and you yourself told me some years ago that the expensive craftsmen at John Lobb have been your family's cobbler for several generations."

"And what makes you think I'm here on some errand for the royal family or that I'm planning to visit Lady Forsythia today?"

"According to an urchin in my employ who monitors the comings and goings of all the swells who inhabit Knightsbridge and its fashionable environs, you take tea with Lady Forsythia nearly every Saturday afternoon, as well as some Tuesdays. And as to the royal family, were you not to be observed leaving a side entrance of Buckingham Palace just this morning? I hardly think you were there on a social visit."

"I suppose my visit to the Palace was witnessed by another of your vast network of urchins."

He gave me a smug look and a careless wave of his gloved hand as he withdrew to the curb. I barked at the driver to get underway. I don't mind admitting I was steamed; Holmes had managed to take the edge off the jolly feeling of satisfaction I'd felt upon delivering the Dragusha brothers into the hands of justice.

I called up to the driver, "Buckingham Palace, good sir."

CHAPTER THREE

The prince came into his drawing room wearing a dressing gown.

"You are back so soon," he said. "Kudlow says you have news for me. It's caused me to interrupt my bath. I hope it's important."

"I wanted to rush back to report to you today, Your Highness, rather than making you fret another day."

"Very well. What is your news?"

"Case closed," I said. "I have dispatched the two brothers into the care of the police, and all without a breath of your name entering the conversation."

"By Jove," he said. "That's absolutely splendid."

"There is one small problem remaining, one that depends for its resolution on your royal cooperation," I said.

"Please tell me," he said.

"The girl has to go."

He blinked rapidly, his jaw hanging low. Finally he croaked, "Why?" "Put simply, she's a shill, a plant, a charlatan—pure, 100% mountebank."

"What?" he sputtered, staggering slightly. "I can scarcely believe what you are saying."

"You must believe it," I said. "When I was here this morning I deduced that she was not Bulgarian and not likely to be their sister. I confirmed it with the two brothers this afternoon. I have a signed paper."

"My God," he said, holding his head in his hands. "What shall I do?"

"First, dispatch Kudlow to bring the girl. I should like to confront her and see how she reacts."

The prince rang a bell and Kudlow poked his head in the door. "Your Highness?"

The prince said, "Fetch the girl." He lifted his head up and said to me, "You must think I'm a fool."

"Nothing of the sort," I said. "Your Highness has the weight of the kingdom's welfare on his mind at all times. You need some respite from your duties."

Of course that was utter nonsense, but I didn't want to deprive the man of his dignity. A fellow who has just lost his mistress is in a most vulnerable emotional state.

The prince's chin was trembling. "You said you deduced she was an impostor, Roller. How did you know?"

"I had my suspicions when I saw the extreme pulchritude of the young lady in question. Nobody who looks like that would find her way into household service. But it became plain as day when I heard her speak."

"But how?"

"Her accent is Slovenian, not Bulgarian."

"Good God! How could you know such a thing?"

"It is my business to know such things, Your Highness. In specific, I had the advantage of a leisurely journey through the Balkans some years ago in the company of my late father, during which I developed a keen sensitivity to the varying vocal utterances of the populace."

The prince said, "I cannot conceive of voluntarily visiting the Balkans. What was your father doing in that benighted place?"

"Father traveled often, usually seeking relief from the rigors of matrimony."

"Ah," the prince said, nodding his head in sympathy.

"I whiled away a great deal of time sitting in cafes, waiting for Father to complete his surveys of the local female population. It was there that I picked up the nuances of the languages of the region, plus a lifelong fondness for a well-made cup of coffee."

"Where is that damned Ludlow?" the prince said, his face growing pink with impatience. He snatched up the bell and rang it furiously. A butler galloped in to see what the hoopla was about.

"Find out where Ludlow has gotten to and send him back right away!"

The butler dashed out, but another minute went by without Ludlow appearing, during which the prince fumed and agitated himself in various ways. Finally the door burst open and Ludlow came into the room at a prance, bowing all the way.

"Your Highness! I'm sorry, but the girl is not to be found! We've searched everywhere."

The prince looked at me, helplessness written all over his features. "What shall we do?"

"I'm thinking," I said.

"Your Highness," Ludlow broke in.

The prince hissed at him. "Do not interrupt Sir Errol while he is thinking."

Ludlow bowed and scraped backwards out of the room.

The prince said, "Please share your thoughts with me."

I said, "First off, your Highness could simply say 'Good Riddance' to the girl and never give the whole matter a another thought. What do you think of that path?"

I could see his jaw clenching and unclenching, no doubt attempting to control his emotions. Finally he shook his head. "I cannot do that." He lapsed into silence, continuing to stare into his lap and shake his head in puzzlement.

"Would Your Highness care to tell me why?"

He let out a big sigh. "She always seemed so sincere in her affections. It is hard for me to believe that it was all chicanery."

"The false appearance of sincerity is a skill possessed in great abundance by the typical *poseur*, Your Highness. One should not criticize oneself for falling prey to it."

"That is not all I criticize myself for," he said, leaving a pregnant pause.

"Would Your Highness care to unburden himself?" I asked.

"I suppose I must," he said. He adopted the most sheepish of expressions and said, "Sometimes in a relaxed frame of mind following her tender ministrations I often mused aloud about affairs of state. I got in the habit of confiding in her about sensitive matters."

Oh, my. This was getting richer by the moment.

Suddenly he gave his thigh an emphatic slap. "There's no way around it, Roller. You must find the girl and bring her to me. I have to know the truth about her motives. Perhaps those two brutes forced her into this charade. She herself could well be a victim of these hooligans!"

Ah, the healing balm of self-deception. How good it makes us feel . . . for a time, anyway. His mind could not cope with the possibility that a radiantly beautiful 25-year-old woman could find a paunchy, pale, dreary middle-aged man less than fascinating.

"It is possible, Your Highness, though I feel obliged to warn you . . ."

He held up his hand, forbidding me to continue. "Yes, yes, I understand, but my mind is made up. You must do everything possible to locate the girl so I may speak with her face-to-face."

"Very well, I will turn my full powers to the situation and bring her to Your Highness at the earliest opportunity."

He strode to his desk and brought out a checkbook. He wrote out a check and handed it to me. It was made out to Sir Errol Hyde for the amount of one hundred pounds sterling. "Spare no expense," he said. "Just ask if you need more."

I slipped the check into my pocket and gave the prince a tiny bow, really more of a dipping of my chin.

"Sir Errol," the prince said, an unexpectedly plaintive tone in his voice, "I fear the worst."

His tone penetrated the veil of mild contempt I attempt to maintain when dealing with members of the royal family. I found myself touched by the misery and, dare I say, humility in his voice. I felt an unfamiliar sense of warmth toward the man.

"My dear prince—why do you feel such dark feelings about the matter?"

He let out a sigh so long and burdened that I thought it might never end. He looked up at me from under his brow and said, "Because I am hopelessly in love with the girl."

"One never need feel guilty about love, Your Highness. It is in such short supply that we should celebrate any instance of it, even if it occurs at inconvenient times."

"Thank you, Roller. I knew you would have a fresh outlook on the problem."

"Brighter times are ahead, Your Highness. There is nothing like love to make you think the world is coming to an end, but as our wise elders have told us, 'This too shall pass.' "

The prince did not look wholly convinced, but suddenly I was virtually itching to get out of the royal presence. I wanted to question the girl's closest associates but I decided to do it on another occasion when the tumult had died down. I murmured that perhaps a hot bath would be helpful in easing the prince's tensions, to which suggestion he nodded glumly and shuffled off toward the princely quarters. I legged off in the other direction, eager to get my nose out into the air of London, such as it is.

I gave the carriage driver a generous tip for waiting for me and told him I preferred walking home. The heavens were dark and gorged with imminent rain but I set off at a brisk pace back toward Knightsbridge, armed with my trusty bumbershoot. I do some of my best thinking while on the march. Much pondering was required to develop a plan for recovering the girl. In addition, I was due at Lady Forsythia's house for tea within the hour and I did not wish to have my mind cluttered with workaday matters while attempting polite conversation with my betrothed.

After a quick stop at my flat to refresh myself I hiked the two streets over to Lady Forsythia's and presented myself for tea. Her maid, Myrtle—she of the perpetually disapproving squint—answered the door and led me into the drawing room to await the good Lady's appearance.

As I sat on the sofa I resisted the urge to scratch the itch I felt along my forearms. Sometimes when I contemplate all the good works Lady Forsythia performs in the world I get a sensation under my skin like the imminent outbreak of hives. My clever friend, Otto, who dabbles in the game of psychology, tells me it's because I feel guilty that I do not contribute more to society's wellbeing. He says I compare myself unfavorably with Lady Forsythia in the save-the-world department and punish myself with the itching. I think he may be right, but so far this wisdom hasn't filtered through to my skin.

Moments later my dear Forsythia swept into the room and bathed me in the full radiance of her attention.

"Errol, dear," she trilled, "how lovely to see you!"

"The feeling is entirely mutual, my precious betrothed."

"Will you take tea, my dear Errol?"

Since I'd taken tea with her the previous fifty or so Saturdays, I was never quite sure why she felt compelled to ask me on every visit if I would take tea. However, one could be sure it was part of Lady Forsythia's rigid code of social conduct, a code so complex and multi-faceted that it still remained largely opaque to me.

"Yes, dear Forsythia, I believe I will indeed take tea."

She rang her little bell and moments later the odious Myrtle appeared, her scowl still fully intact.

"We would love some tea, dear Myrtle. And please this time remember that Sir Errol prefers two lumps of sugar, not one."

On numerous occasions Myrtle had fouled up my sugar requirements by exactly half, which I'm sure she did not to trim household expenses, as she claimed but also, as the Americans say, to "get my goat."

Myrtle sniffed disapprovingly and set off to fetch the tea.

Lady Forsythia returned her attention to me, her clear green eyes sparkling. "What exciting adventures has my daring Errol been involved with this week? Please tell something thrilling to a woman who has done nothing but noble charitable works all week long. Do you possibly have a sordid little nugget for your beloved?"

I should mention that Lady Forsythia relied upon me for graphic reports of the seamier side of London life. As part of my ongoing efforts to warm her affections toward me, I tried never to disappoint her.

"Well, there is one matter which has engaged my professional attention of late."

"Oh, goody," she said. "Is it about sex or money? Those are the only two subjects that in my view make proper scandal."

"I think milady might fancy this tale, because it involves both sex AND money."

"I am most raptly attentive, dear Errol."

"Let us say, then, that a certain noble personage has become carnally enraptured with a young lady who serves below stairs."

"Oh, my word! Please continue," Lady Forsythia said, a tiny hint of pink rising above the pristine white collar of her blouse.

"And if I may give further detail, this fascination has found expression in the young servant's frequent visits to his quarters, there to engage in sensual acts which the noble personage's lawfully wedded wife will not perform, finding them off-putting in the extreme."

Lady Forsythia's eyes widened. "Are we talking bums and gums?"

"Quite!" I said, marveling inwardly at Lady Forsythia's grasp of the vernacular. "But that's not the whole of the problem."

Her hand flew to her mouth. "Oh dear! Has the noble personage also strayed into more fertile territory, resulting in the impregnation of this talented young woman, this nymph whose skills appear to go somewhat beyond the usual requirements of household staff?"

"No, thankfully there is no spare heir to contend with, but there were certain complications that required a brief sojourn by myself to the dank byways of Whitechapel."

Lady Forsythia gasped, no doubt shocked at hearing the name of that foul place uttered in the pristine serenity of her drawing room. I noticed a deeper flush of pink creeping up her neckline and asked her ladyship if I should continue.

"Oh, yes!" she said, her breath coming rapidly.

"Very well, then I shall. To follow a fruitful clue I was forced to enter one of those awful, dim-lit taverns in which the denizens of that mean mile congregate."

"No! It cannot be true that you have seen the interior of such a foul place! Please describe it in great detail."

"True it is, my dear lady! Oh, how murky and hellishly awful it was, redolent with the stench of every imaginable excrescence hovering over the dizzying smell of beer and cheap gin. And in those dark environs I came face-to-face with two brothers, bulky of heft and Balkan of birth, who threatened me with bodily harm."

"Good God, Errol. Please go on. I'm more than eager to hear how you dealt with these bulky Balkans, especially how you managed to handle their aggression while remaining completely unscathed."

So eager was she to hear my story that she was virtually squirming in her chair.

"Before I go on, my darling betrothed, may I make a modest observation?"

"Of course, dear Errol, so long as it does not retard for long the building momentum of your adventure."

"I note, precious Forsythia, that your throat has become flushed and your breathing has escalated during the telling of my story. I would suggest that if we added an actual physical embrace to the equation you might feel the joys of even greater arousal."

Suddenly her brows narrowed into an expression of disapproval that bordered on the Myrtle-esque.

"Errol, have you perchance been smoking hashish again?"

Drat it all! Snared like a rabbit! Lady Forsythia's virtues were so refined that she could discern improprieties the ordinary person would never perceive.

I ducked my head to show a little remorse. "In the spirit of maintaining the flow of open communication between us, so essential a quality to maintain between two people of good will during a lengthy courtship, I must confess that I had a small puff before dropping by."

She shook her head sadly. "I suspected as such. Only a person in the grip of a heady intoxicant would propose such a premature and headlong leap into the physical expression of our betrothal."

"I merely thought that we might perhaps embrace lightly while I whispered the rest of the story into that pink little ear of yours."

"Sir Errol!"

"My apologies, dearest. I lost my head for a moment."

"The effects of that foreign herb you persist in imbibing, no doubt."

"No doubt," I said.

At that moment Myrtle barged through the door bearing a tray of tea items, and conversation quickly bobbed to the surface. Lady Forsythia was never able to shrug off her miff, and so I departed after tea with nothing but a slightly stiff neck to show for our time together.

Fortunately, that's why our Benevolent Creator saw fit to give us hot baths, and after returning to my flat I drew a deep one, added a generous amount of the wintergreen-scented bath salts I favor, and sank into the water to seek relief, aided in my quest for serenity by another pipe-full of the herb to which Lady Forsythia had such opposition, ill-informed though I believed her position to be. Soon I was in a better frame of mind and able to muster my resources. In fact, I soon found myself in such a tip-top mood that my refreshed mind produced a flow of new ideas about how to proceed with the prince's case.

After bathing I dressed again and set off into the evening to do a spot more of detecting.

CHAPTER FOUR

I presented myself at the headquarters of the constabulary and greeted the desk sergeant. The sergeant had obviously heard of my donation to the widows and orphans fund, because he sprang to his feet and came around the desk to clasp my hand.

"Sir Errol, what a pleasure to see you! How may we serve you?"

"Is Inspector Dinwoodie gracing the premises this evening?"

"I fear not, sir. He has gone home to wife and family."

"As it should be," I said. "I came to ask his permission to interview the two men he incarcerated earlier in the afternoon."

"Ah, yes, the two burly brothers."

"Exactly."

"I'm sure the inspector would extend every courtesy to a gentleman of good intent such as yourself. Please follow me and I will escort you to where the two rapscallions are resting their considerable bulk."

I followed him at a brisk place down a flight of stairs into the basement, where he unlocked the massive door and ushered me into a block of holding cells. It was not an unfamiliar place to me—I'd conducted interviews with other guests of the department—but I cringed once again at the din of noise and the thick miasma of odors emanating from the cells.

"Not a fit place for a gentleman," the sergeant said. "Let me bring the two miscreants out to the interrogation room so you won't have to endure the catcalls of the cutpurses, hooligans and other doers of evil deeds we have collected here."

That was fine with me. I withdrew to the room and waited in its bare interior until he returned with the two brothers, securely handcuffed. They had apparently been napping, because they stumbled into the room grumbling and blinking their eyes. Something else was quite apparent, too: they'd both been given a righteous thrashing. Both their faces were lumpy and red-blotched. The brother with the drooping moustache was now adorned also with a drooping right eye, swollen and ringed with a shiny, black bruise.

The sergeant said, "When we locked them up they were blathering something about the royal family so we had to give them a bit of discipline to shut them up." He pushed them roughly into the two chairs that sat across the table from my chair.

"Would you like me to remain in the room with you, Sir Errol?"

"I'll be just fine, Sergeant. Please stand by outside. I shan't be long."

The sergeant withdrew and I surveyed the two ruffians, whose brief period of incarceration had not improved either their moods or the rank vapors that emanated from them.

"Whaddaya want?" the bearded brother asked.

"The question, my good fellow, is what do YOU want?"

"Hunh?"

"I can help make your stay with the police much more comfortable if you will answer a few questions of mine."

Moustache said, "You already tricked us once, getting us to sign that paper and all."

I said, "Did I not tell you that learning to read English would be advantageous for you? Perhaps you could see my so-called trickery as inspiration to learn how to read our fine language while you are reposing as guests of His Majesty. It would open up new worlds for you. You would, for example, be able to sample the infinite riches of Shakespeare, our beloved bard."

"Fuck your bard," Beard said.

Now that's a sentiment you don't hear every day! However, in the spirit of honesty I must confess that on occasion, fighting back yawns in the fourth or fifth or sixth act of some interminable tragedy Lady Forsythia had dragged me to, I had fleetingly entertained that same notion myself.

So much for my attempts to improve their lot through education! I got to my main point: "I need to know anything and everything about your colleague, Ariana. Where did she come from? Whose idea was it to fleece the prince? Where is she to be found? Answer my questions forthrightly and I'll see to it that your stay here is much more comfortable."

"How are you gonna do that?" Moustache demanded to know.

"I'll show you," I said. I got out two gold sovereigns from my pocket. "I told you before you were arrested that you would get some gold, and I plan to make good on that promise."

Beard pointed to the coins. "What're we gonna do with that in here?"

"Shut up," his brother said. "Let him talk."

"If I were you, I'd tuck it in a damp, dark place on your person and only remove it at times of daily necessity."

He stared at me dully.

"He means up your ass," Moustache said.

Beard grunted.

"Plus, I'll put in a word upstairs that will get you released after 30 days. You'll walk out of here rested and refreshed. Tidy up your sovereign a bit and you'll have a solid gold start on your future."

Moustache said, "What do you want to know?"

"Whose idea was the scam?"

"A guy with a mask. We never saw his face."

"What kind of a mask? Just a plain black one or one with a face on it?"

"That feller with the bonfire and all."

That bonfire? I was momentarily stumped, but then it dawned on me that they were referring to the annual bonfire that commemorates the successful foiling of the Gunpowder Plot."

"Guy Fawkes?" I asked.

"Yeah, the feller with the moustache and pointy beard."

"Very well, he was wearing a Guy Fawkes mask. Where did this take place?"

"Some fancy house outside the city. They brought us out there in a carriage. It was first time I ever been in one and it made me sick to my stomach."

Beard piped up with a chuckle, "Heaved right out the carriage window, he did." He made a louder cackle, savoring the memory. "And he'd had oysters for dinner! Jeez, now that was a sight!"

Based on what I'd seen so far, the Bulgarian sense of humor was not of the subtle variety. I asked Moustache what the masked man's instructions were.

"All we had to do was rough the butler up and give him a piece of paper."

"And how much did he pay you for this service?"

"Half a crown."

Half a crown for the both of them! I felt a slight twinge that I was overpaying them lavishly by giving them a sovereign each, but I decided it was not quite the right time to haggle.

"Did you meet the girl at that time?"

"Yeah, the woman brought her in."

"The woman? What did she look like?"

He shrugged "She were a squat little thing. She had a mask on, too."

"What kind?"

His face bunched up. "I don't rightly know what to call it. Wasn't like nothing I'd ever seen before. Scary-like."

I didn't know what to make of that. "Did the girl help plan this thing?"

They both laughed.

"She very stupid," Beard said, causing my mind to seize up momentarily. Given his minimal level of intellectual capacity, the fact that he considered the girl dim-witted took stupidity into a dimension with which I was not familiar.

"She was Slovenian," Moustache added helpfully.

Beard slapped his thigh. "Hey, maybe that's why they're called Slow-venians!" He threw back his head and croaked out a phlegm-y laugh.

This confirmed my suspicion about the Bulgarian sense of humor.

During my brief conversation with the girl she had not seemed particularly slow-witted. "What did she do that made you think she was stupid? After all, you only met her that one time."

"She weren't even getting paid!" Moustache said.

"Tell me more."

"I figured she had to be getting more than a half-crown like we were, so I asked her what she was getting paid. She just gave me a nasty look and said she had other reasons."

Beard said, "If that ain't stupid I don't know what is."

I gave the table a sharp slam with my hand. "Snap to, damn it! Just answer my questions. And, by the way, if you breathe one word of any of this to anyone I'll see to it that you spend the next year inside one of those cells."

"You got nothin' to worry about," Moustache said, "You got the gold. You're the guv'nor. We ain't saying a word."

"All right. So you don't have any idea where she is?"

They both shook their heads.

"Well, then, let's go back to the beginning. How did they contact you in the first place?"

"A guy down at the Bulgarian Social Hall said somebody was looking for muscle. Said if we were interested we were supposed to go see a cabbie and he'd take us out to the house."

"Did you know the guy?"

They shook their heads again. "He wasn't even Bulgarian. He just came in one day and saw us, said we'd do."

"Was he a gentleman or a man of the people?"

"Sort of halfway in between."

"What do you mean?"

"One of them fellows what wears a bowler hat."

"A butler?"

"Yeah, like that."

"And what were his instructions to you?"

"He said there was a half-crown in it for five minutes work. He gave us a down payment of a shilling each and a pint of ale and told us which cabbie to see to get the ride out there."

"Where did you meet this cabbie?"

"He was in the cab line outside a posh hotel over by Hyde Park."

"Really!" That was my neighborhood. Indeed, before old Henry VIII acquired the property and named it Hyde Park it was called Hyde Manor, the original stomping grounds of my clan. The vast fortune of the Hyde family had been made on the sale of the old manor to the crown. The fortune had remained abundant through generations until my father got hold of it and deflated it through his passion for baccarat and his largesse with ex-wives.

Father's marriages were never lengthy affairs. Once his fascination wore off—which typically took from one to three years—he was always so eager to be rid of his wives that he made outlandishly lavish settlements on them. The pittance he left for me is just barely enough to maintain the modest degree of luxury required of a gentleman of my station and, of course, to keep me from having to work for a living.

I asked the brothers, "Do you remember the name of the hotel?"

Beard shook his head, but Moustache scrunched up his face in the effort to remember. "It was the name of some posh," he said.

That narrowed it down but not by much. I suggested, "The Barkley?"

He shook his head.

"Cubberly?"

"No, longer-sounding."

"How about Dillingham's?"

He bobbed his head. "Yeah, that was it."

Ha! The episode had taken place scarcely two blocks from my flat. I'd passed the carriage line out in front of Dillingham's dozens of time, never once suspecting that such nefarious schemes were a-brew.

"I want to talk to that cabbie. Can you describe him to me?"

"Yeah, he were a little fellow with a bad eye, name of Charlie."

Would that all witnesses could be so succinct! I called for the sergeant to return the brothers to their cell and pressed five shillings into his hand for his trouble. His face broke into a smile, of a magnitude normally reserved for greeting one's mother after a long absence. "Thank YOU, Sir Errol. Is there anything else I can do for you?"

"Those fellows were very helpful to me. Please tell Inspector Dinwoodie I hope he goes easy on them. Could you ask the Inspector to call on me at his leisure?"

"I'll have the Inspector call on you at his earliest opportunity, Sir Errol."

"No hurries, my good man. I think I have everything I need."

CHAPTER FIVE

Half an hour later I was surveying the cab line in front of Dillingham's. Three carriages were waiting, but none of the drivers had wonky eyes or were "little fellows."

"I say," calling up to the cabbie in the first carriage. "Is Charlie on duty today?"

He shook his head. "Charlie don't come on 'til nine this evening."

An hour; it was just enough time to get a quick bite to eat before he arrived. I ducked into Dillingham's and strode across the lobby to the dining room. There were only a few diners scattered here and there in the big room; the Maitre D came scurrying toward me with a menu and a grateful look in his eye.

"Top of the evening to you, sir. May we offer you sustenance?"

"That is my fondest hope, dear fellow." I followed him to a table near the window. I perused the menu and found a few items that looked promising. I ordered a lamb chop and roast potatoes. English cuisine has its detractors; I myself have been heard to utter a carp or two about the over-reliance on Brussels sprouts and the tendency to skimp on desserts. However, in the realm of the lamb chop the English chef has no equal.

When the sommelier came around I consulted with him at length, finally restricting myself to a half-bottle of the 1900 vintage Chateau Margaux. I needed to keep all my faculties keen for when Charlie clopped onto the scene.

While I waited for my food to arrive I busied myself with the pocket edition of Ovid I often carry with me. I was mid-way through

Book Two, where the going gets a little heavy for a fellow whose last Latin tutorial was twenty years ago. However, as my scholarly Uncle Lemuel was always wont to say, "A gentleman must always keep his Latin sharp," so I pressed on regardless of the pain and suffering.

This very issue had led to a snippy bit of repartee between Holmes and myself, resulting in the cessation of discourse between us for several months. A few years ago I had stopped by the flower shop inside The Connaught Hotel to pick up a certain type of yellow tea rose I savor, to be used as my opening bid for an affectionate evening with the lovely and luscious Helga von Munchen. The flower shop in the august lobby of The Connaught is the only place I know that offers that variety of rose.

To my surprise I saw Holmes, dressed to the nines, sitting alone with a small book clutched to hand. When I approached him to exchange a pleasantry I noted that he hastily stuffed the book in his pocket. I showed him my pocket edition of Ovid and asked him what he was reading. Somewhat reluctantly, or so it seemed to me, he extracted a battered pocket edition of Seneca and displayed it. Did I note a trace of sheepishness?

I peered at it and saw it was an English translation. I felt a sweet breeze of glee blow through the steamy dominions of my belly.

"Do you read Seneca?" he asked.

"Certainly," I said, "but of course not in English; it is so much more powerful in the original Latin." In all honesty, I may have put a bit more archness in my tone than was absolutely necessary.

He took it poorly and came back at me with a barb, opining as follows: "I thought Ovid rather a waste of time."

I simply could not allow that to stand, so I lobbed a swat of my own back at him. "I'm not surprised," I said. "Ovid is about the art of love. Relationships, especially with the opposite sex, do not appear to be a focus of your singularly brilliant mind."

He was sputtering to reply when Dr. Watson stumped up, apologizing profusely for being late. After greeting the good doctor I politely withdrew and left them to their tea.

I was savoring the memory of that moment when the waiter came bearing my lamb chop. It was sizzling and juicy, revealing a perfect pink interior. The potatoes were redolent with rosemary, crisp on the outside and creamy-soft on the inside, just the way I like them. As for the wine, I've never met a Margaux I didn't like, and this one did not disappoint. It was floral yet earthy, with truffle and tobacco bass notes graced by cedar-wood inflections on the long finish.

So went my hour of waiting for Charlie to come on duty. After polishing off a bit of toffee pudding I paid for my dinner, bringing tears to my waiter's eyes with a few extra shillings tip for him. He assured me that he and his fourteen children would use it wisely, especially now that the wife was lying-in with number fifteen. I silently gave thanks again that our Benevolent Creator had not blessed me with offspring. The Hyde family had given it a darned good run, a few hundred years worth, and I saw no harm in letting the breed peter out, as it were.

Outside I braced myself against the chill air. A desperate wind was beginning to howl down the canyons of the city in anticipation of the storm coming behind it. I heard a bell chime once, signaling a quarter past the hour, as I scanned the cab line looking for my man. And there he was at the end of the line, huddled in the driver's seat bundled to the gills, clutching his hat to his head against the wind. He had a patch over his left eye.

I went down the line to his cab and called up to him. "Charlie?"

He jerked upright, probably surprised at hearing me call him by name. "Sir?"

"I'd like to talk to you about one of your recent fares." I offered a half-crown up to him, probably more money than he would make all night. His eyes widened to the size of poker chips.

"Why, thank you, sir! What would you like to know?"

"Can we get inside your cab? You look a bit chilly up there."

He clambered down and opened the carriage door for me. I climbed in and got myself situated. Although not balmy by any means, the interior of the cab at least kept us out of the wind, now blowing hard enough to rock the carriage.

"Bound to be a foul night, Sir!" he said.

I pointed to where the coin I'd given him was now clasped securely in his hand. "But now you have the means to spend at least part of it in a nice, warm tavern." And invest a few pence in a bath and laundry while you're at it, I added mentally, not wanting to spoil the moment by suggesting that his odor of sweat and horse manure was anything but pleasing to my nose.

"Aye, sir. I'm very grateful. How may I serve you?"

"I want to know about two people you took out of the city. Two big Bulgarian brothers."

He flinched and shrunk back into the seat. "Oh, no. I cannot!"

"What do you mean?"

"They said if I ever mentioned it they'd come find me and cut off my hands."

"Who told you that? The brothers?"

He shook his head violently. "The woman! The woman in the mask!"

The little fellow was quaking like a leaf, and it wasn't due to the cold. He looked terrified.

"Now, Charlie. Please don't fret. I have very good news for you. The two brothers have been imprisoned and the whole matter is under investigation. Just answer my questions and I will guarantee nobody will ever learn of this from me."

I jingled a few coins in my hand, suggesting the possibility of future remuneration. The sound had a salubrious effect on his anxiety.

"All right, m'lord," he said, pulling himself out of his cringe.

"Stout fellow! Now, give me the address of the house." I didn't want to ask the poor fellow to take me out there himself, so I handed him a piece of paper and a pen and asked him to write it down.

He dipped his head. "Begging your pardon, m'lord, I never learned how."

I restrained the urge, noble as it was, to instruct Charlie on the practical and moral value of mastering the King's English in its written form.

"Then tell me where the house is."

He described a location in Oxfordshire, not far from Blenheim Palace. "How long by carriage?" I asked.

"I wouldn't recommend it on a foul night like this, m'lord."

"No, no, I mean how long did it take with the brothers?"

"Best part of six hours, sir. A bit faster coming back, the horses wanting to get home to their dinner and such."

Good lord! A dozen hours in a horse-drawn carriage! Perhaps the brothers had already received punishment enough. The masked and mysterious couple must have had some good reason for not bringing the brothers out on the train; it was not only less painful but less expensive as well.

I couldn't think of anything else I wanted to ask Charlie, so I bid him farewell, reassuring him once again that I would keep his observations in strictest confidence. Rain was beginning to pelt the carriage in earnest, making me resist stepping out into the night. Suddenly an idea gripped me.

"I say, Charlie, would you be kind enough to run me around to Basil Street?" It was only three blocks away but I was keen on arriving at my destination looking my best.

"Sadly, sir, I cannot. You must go to the first cab in the line. If I jumped my place in line I'd get a thrashing from the other drivers."

"What! Because of some arbitrary law of cab drivers I have to get wet and chilled to the bone?"

"My apologies, m'lord. Perhaps if your lordship would consider a tip to the other drivers they'd let me go."

"How much?"

"A shilling each should do it, sir."

I handed him three shillings and he went out into the howling wind to dispense them to the cabbies in front of us. A minute or two later, the palms of the other drivers suitably lubricated, we went rattling off to Basil Street. When we arrived at my destination I gave Charlie a couple more shillings and asked him to walk me to the door with his umbrella. It was only ten feet to the shelter of the porch but the rain was now coming down in sheets. We clambered out of the carriage and dashed up the steps. Charlie, being a head shorter than I, got well soaked, but fortunately I was spared the brunt of it.

"Please wait, Charlie. If my friend isn't home I will require a lift to my flat."

"Very good, sir." He dashed back to the safety of the carriage.

I pressed the big brass button and heard the chime inside. Presently I saw an approaching figure through the fogged window. I signaled to Charlie that he could leave and put on my most bashful smile to greet Helga von Munchen, my guide and confessor.

The door opened and the lady in question regarded me with an amused smile. "Errol!" she said. "Or must I call you *Sir* Errol now that you've joined the ranks of Sir Lancelot and other defenders of the kingdom?"

I knew I was in for a drubbing, so I ducked my head to signal my submission.

"Errol will do just fine. May I come in?"

"You actually want to come into my house? To visit *me*?" she said, needling me a bit more with her trademark sarcasm, the barbed and mordant nature of which was much admired in London social circles. She opened the door wide and welcomed me into the snug warmth of the house. She helped me off with my coat and hung it on the rack.

"Now, Helga, please don't be too hard on me. I've just come in from truly dreadful weather."

She chuckled. "He begs me not to be too hard. That's very humorous, especially since you used to beg me so often to *get* you hard!"

"Helga, dear, how I've missed you. No other woman can make me feel so constantly wrong."

"Ah, Errol. No other man is so in need of being constantly reminded how very wrong he is."

She continued to cane me lightly with such utterances all the way into the drawing room, where she rang for her manservant, Rattigan, to bring us libations.

"I still have a drop or two of the hundred-year-old cognac you once fancied," she said. "Could you be persuaded to entertain a sip?"

"Indeed I would. A tiny snifter of that elixir would please me deeply."

"And what about the fifty-year-old woman you used to fancy? Do your evening plans include a drop or two of her elixir on your not-unskilled tongue?"

Helga was not one to insist on a great deal of social conversation before getting down to the nub of the matter. Fortunately just then old Rattigan shuffled into the room, sparing me having to declare my intentions.

"Evening, sir." He bowed to me then turned to Helga for his instructions, which she gave and sent him on his way to fulfill.

It had been a year since I'd seen Helga, but time had treated her most kindly. She was statuesque, in the German way, fronted generously of bosom and beamish of bottom. The word *voluptuous* is seldom used anymore but it happened to fit Helga as well as the peignoir and cashmere robe that draped so languidly over her curves. I had come to her house for conversational purposes but I could feel stirrings of another nature occurring far below the level of polite discourse.

Helga leaned forward and put her hand on my knee. "If I may be permitted an observation, dear Errol, you look a bit riled up this evening. What has got Sir Errol's mainspring wound so tightly?"

I had never been able to maintain any sort of pretense with Helga, so I blurted it right out: "I took tea today with Lady Forsythia."

"Ah," she said. "Say no more." She shrugged slightly, causing the cashmere robe to slip off her shoulders, revealing the swell and cleavage of her creamy-white bosom. I was transfixed, wishing very much to bury my nose in those warm and inviting depths.

"Perhaps the good knight needs to have his jousting-pole polished a bit before he can settle down and tell Helga what's on his mind."

As usual, her penetrating awareness captured my very mood; I let her take me by the hand and lead me toward the stairs I'd mounted so many times. Old Rattigan rattled up with our drinks, which we carried with us up to her bedroom. There, I was delighted to discover that both the 100-year-old cognac and the 50-year-old woman had both aged magnificently.

(Dear Reader, I hope you will not be disappointed by my reticence in describing the clinical details of lovemaking. I know that I could probably attract a larger readership if I were to use the kind of phraseology popular in pulp fiction, sentences such as "When she climaxed it was like a thousand Roman candles went off over the Coliseum" and "He exploded in her with an intensity that made her eardrums bulge out." I was schooled, however, at the knee of my beloved Grandmother Hyde, who instructed me relentlessly in life's fundamentals. In her words, "A gentleman never discusses money, or God forbid, sex." I've liberalized her teachings slightly to allow myself to discuss those subjects, but only when absolutely necessary.)

Suffice it to say that my lovemaking with Helga was as languorous as the drape of her peignoir and as thrilling as the piercing clarity of her azure eyes. Afterwards she drew us a hot bath, scented with the lemon bath salts she favored, and we luxuriated among the bubbles to the sound of Strauss waltzes playing softly on the gramophone.

"Would you like another drop of cognac?" Helga asked.

"Thank you, no. I have achieved a most favorable glow."

"Then talk to me, Errol. Share your burdens with me as you so often have done."

I should mention that my rich history with Madame von Munchen began when I was a mere lad of nineteen and Helga a worldly thirty-year-old. I was home for the holidays in my sophomore year at Cambridge when my father one day spotted a fresh pimple sprouting on my forehead.

"Ugly business, those dratted spots on your face," he said, with his trademark lack of sensitivity to all things adolescent.

"Yes," I admitted, "I get those from time to time. Bloody nuisance."

"And have you ever considered why you get them?" he asked.

"I have been told that it is a typical symptom of the stage of life I'm in. Other people my age also seem to struggle with them."

"Nonsense," he said. "That's utter rot. These spots, which so disgrace your noble countenance, the remarkable features of which are the result of ten generations of good breeding, are caused by the absence of a robust sex life."

Really! "Then I guess I come by them honestly, Father. My sex life is particularly un-robust."

"I thought as much," he said, clucking sympathetically. "Well, we shall see what we can do about that."

The next evening he gave me a quick lecture on matters of hygiene and delivered me to the front door of a fine grey-stone house on Basil Street in Knightsbridge.

"I have made certain arrangements," Father said cryptically, as he pressed the brass knob of the doorbell. "Think of it as an early birthday present."

The door opened and I beheld for the first time the sympathetic face and voluptuous body of Helga von Munchen. Dressed in a flowing red velvet gown, she was magnificently corseted and cantilevered so that her lily-white bosom soared forward at an angle one seldom sees in nature.

On the subject of bosoms, I feel called to part the veil of memory for a moment to explain my lifelong fascination with those shimmering, beckoning orbs to which medical textbooks refer so prosaically as "mammary glands." When I made my appearance in the world, so hungry in my body for sustenance, my mother had recently decided to give my father the boot. She can't be blamed; she lasted longer than most of them. As I got to know Old Dad better I was always amazed she could bear to be around him for a full three years.

In any case, I'm told she tried to nurse me for a month or so but couldn't produce the required nutrients. She then threw in the towel and decamped for St. Tropez. Sadly, our paths never again crossed. Much later Father told me that her untimely death by drowning, mere months after her departure, came while playing the new sport of water polo. I was turned over to a succession of bottle-wielding nannies that managed the household and me during Father's frequent absences. (And speaking of turnover, the rate was high among the nannies because several were fired, I would later find out, for resisting my father's attempts to lure them into bed.)

Just a few years ago I got myself into a bit of a *contretemps* when accompanying Lady Forsythia to the Covent Garden Opera. She reprimanded me for gazing too long and deeply into the cleavage of the opera-lover seated next to us. I believe the exact phrase she hissed into my ear was, "Stop staring at her tits."

In the aftermath of this regrettable incident Lady Forsythia insisted I go all the way to Zurich to visit the esteemed Dr. Jung, whose ideas were just then beginning to sweep fashionable London. It was her contention that the good doctor could rid me of what she considered an unhealthy fascination. To keep from making waves I went along with her scheme, even though I, like any sensible Englishman, knew there couldn't possibly be anything to gain from visiting Switzerland. I was also firmly of the belief that Lady Forsythia's obsession in regard to this matter was not entirely due to my flawed nature. It was my contention that she was angry with our Benevolent Creator for His decision to gift her somewhat stingily in the breast department.

Jung turned out to be insufferably bumptious. He prattled on for two sessions about my "archetype" and other daft notions, then gave up and sent me on my way, citing his difficulties in penetrating what he called my "thick persona." He also over-charged me mercilessly.

I hope, Dear Reader, you will take heed from my cautionary tale and be at your most wary anytime someone, particularly a romantic partner, suggests you change anything about yourself.

At age nineteen, standing on Helga's front steps, I couldn't muster words to greet Helga properly, so focused was my attention on the burgeoning activities below my belt.

Helga said to my father, "Peregrine Hyde, you old dog! You didn't tell me this young gentleman of yours was so gorgeous to look at!"

Father muttered his thanks and climbed back in the carriage, no doubt in a hurry to tuck in to the rich feast of his own evening. Helga drew me into herself with a big hug, pressing her bosom up under my chin, and I was thus welcomed into the warmth of her hospitality.

It was far and away the most splendid acne cure ever devised. I went back to Cambridge for the next term, free of facial blemishes and with a pleasing lightness in my step.

Now, twenty years later, sitting across from her in the delicious environs of her tub, I marveled that she did not look a day older than when I first saw her.

"Don't let me interrupt your rapturous gaze, dear Errol, but please tell me what was troubling you when you first arrived tonight. What conundrum was causing the still waters of your mind to churn so unsettlingly? Is it the matter of Lady Forsythia's uncharitable approach to your manly needs? Or is there something perhaps deeper—perhaps even not connected to the good lady—that sends those worry-ripples across the serene sea of your inner world?"

By Jove, she'd done it again! I said, "Dear Helga, I have begun to suspect the very same thing! I had complained so frequently about Lady Forsythia's seeming lack of interest in my passionate suit that it was beginning to annoy even me. So I asked myself, if Lady Forsythia welcomed me into her bed and ravished me most satisfyingly, would I still be troubled? And the answer was 'Yes.' "

"So then what is it, Errol? What wrinkles the unlined expanses of the noble Hyde forehead?"

"That is what I have not been able to surmise, Helga. Earlier this evening I was seized by the idea that perhaps you could help me cut through this Gordian knot of a knicker-twist I've got myself into."

She nodded. "In our brief time together I've observed two factors that were not at play in you when last we met."

"Ah, so! What are they?"

"Beginning at the top and working downward, one cannot help but notice the distinguished twinges of gray that have begun to grace your flowing locks."

"Yes, I myself had observed that a dash or two of salt had appeared amongst the pepper."

"Perhaps more like a handful than a dash," she added, quite unnecessarily I thought.

"Please, Helga. Do go on."

"And in our love-making this evening, it took a bit longer than usual to coax the stallion out of the stable and deliver him to the starting gate. In times past your prancing thoroughbred was often through the gate before the bell had rung."

"Your point being . . ."

She chuckled. "You're always so thoughtfully quick to point out the foibles of others, dear Errol, so it always surprises me to see how sluggish you can be in perceiving your own."

"Whatever point you are driving at continues to elude me, Helga."

She gave out a long, exasperated sigh and said, "Damn it, Errol, don't you see? You're about to turn 40. You're afraid of getting old!"

I started to interrupt her but she gestured pointedly for me to keep my mouth shut.

"Wait," she said, "it gets worse. The fear of getting old is just a wink of the real fear, which is that you are going to die in the not-too-distant future. This very, actual body of yours is going to suck in a last breath, rattle it out and expire."

Again I tried to get a word in but she shushed me once more. "Wait," she said, "it gets worse. When that moment comes—when you finally do the old suck-and-rattle—you're probably going to leave undone a great many things you still want to do. You just need to make sure you don't leave undone the biggest thing you want to do."

I'm not ashamed to say that her words pole-axed me. Grandmother Hyde would have been horrified had she seen how my jaw hung open for a long second or two before I was able to muster the muscle-power to get it properly clenched again. It was Grandmother's contention that a gentleman's jaw should remain lightly clenched at all times, especially when speaking.

"Helga, you've once again stunned me with your wisdom, such that I cannot begin to mount my usual resistance to it."

"Thank Heaven for that," she said, in a tone of voice that seemed to signal that humor was intended.

"This fear of getting old ... is it something you have faced also, dear Helga?"

She shook her head in a manner that appeared to express wonderment, though I wasn't quite sure what caused this look of amused amazement on her face. "Of course I have, you silly fool! Everybody does. Only most people don't talk about it openly. Instead they spend their time exchanging gossip and buying things they don't need and having silly affairs, simply because they're afraid to face the utterly obvious."

"But Helga! If we aren't gossiping and buying things and having affairs, how would those of us in the upper classes occupy our time?"

"Errol, you have a finely-polished mind and an education at one of the world's great universities. It puzzles me deeply how you can also sometimes be thick as a plank!"

I don't mind telling you, had anyone else said something so bold to me I would have punched him in the snout. Or at the very least given him a hard stare. But with Helga there was never any point in resisting the rattan cane of her wisdom on my metaphorical bottom. I had voluntarily submitted to being in her presence, with all the possibilities that entails, so if I got the privilege of sitting in hot water with her, watching her buoyant breasts a-bob in the water between us, by God I guess I could bend over and take a light caning.

"I feel myself wanting to say 'Helga, whatever do you mean?' But a wiser, though unfamiliar part of me senses you are after something of a deeper nature. I hark back to a statement you made a few moments ago, something to the effect that I should not shrink from asking myself what above all I must do with my life."

She bathed me in a radiant smile, which took away some of the stirrings of anxiety I felt deep inside me.

I said, "Do you have any idea what that is?"

Helga threw back her head and laughed, sending a thoroughly agreeable ripple through the breast-buoys between us. "No, of course not! And even if I did it wouldn't matter in the slightest. It's one of those things you must figure out by yourself."

"One of those things? You mean there are others?"

She had a right guffaw to that, which in Helga's particular style comes out as a series of gasping snorts. When she caught her breath she said, "Heavens, Errol—no one amuses me like you do."

The water in the tub was beginning to cool, along with my ardor. Damn these philosophical questions! I'll say this: if you want to take the stiffness out of a fellow's member, just start asking him about what he wants to do with the precious and ever-shortening number of days allotted to him. Helga's withering insights were having a quite literal withering effect on me: my manly appendage was limp as a windsock on a breezeless day. It made me wonder if perhaps there was some hitherto-unsuspected connection between my brain and my penis, however far-fetched that idea might seem.

But enough of that! I hauled my body out of the bath and dried myself off, leaving Helga to bob amongst the bubbles alone.

"I think I'll stay in here a bit longer," she said. "Can you find your own way out?"

"I can, dear Helga. Thank you for the stimulating evening and thoroughly enlightening conversation."

She chuckled. "Our enlightening conversation appears to have thoroughly darkened your mood, dear Errol."

It was true. Too much wisdom consumed all at once can give one a case of mental indigestion. I needed some time to ponder the issues Helga had stirred up in me. I kissed Helga goodnight and bundled up against the chill. Thankfully the pouring rain had slacked off in favor of a soft drizzle, so I was able to walk the few blocks back to my flat without getting doused. Soon I was snugly tucked in my own bed, where a puff off my pipe and a few pages of Thomas Hardy put me into a deep and dreamless sleep far beyond the reaches of my restless mind.

CHAPTER SIX

The storm passed on through during the night and I awoke the next day to an unfamiliar sight: sunshine streaming through my bedroom window. My dark mood of the night before had disappeared along with the storm clouds, leaving my mind uncluttered and focused only on getting a good cup of coffee inside me at the earliest opportunity. Fortunately I had that aspect of life well covered.

I pulled the little cord that rings the bell in the flat below mine inhabited by my tenant and part-time housekeeper, Francesca. I pictured the lithe and graceful Francesca, dressed in her morning caftan, grinding the beans and pouring boiling water into the French press. Among the many skills in Francesca's repertoire was the ability to make a truly superb cup of coffee.

My tenant had come to London from her native Tuscany to serve as an *au pair* in a grand house in the countryside, only to run afoul of some silly moral turpitude clause in the terms of her employment. As I heard it, the randy patriarch of the manse was slipping Francesca a few extra sovereigns to perform certain manual ministrations upon him, a practice to which the matriarch of the house expressed great displeasure when she caught our girl red-handed, so to speak. They put her on the next train to London.

Rescuing orphans is not usually my style, but when the orphan is twenty-four, gorgeous and ripe as a Maraschino cherry it makes charity a bit more palatable. My old Cambridge friend, Toddy, braced me up one day at the club, interrupting my snooker game to tell me of Francesca's plight and suggesting that my empty flat would be an ideal place of refuge while she got herself established in the city.

Soon the grateful young lady was ensconced a mere ten feet below me, most eager to compensate me for my generosity. Besides making excellent coffee she did a bit of light tidying up and occasionally made late-night mercy-visits when tensions I accrued during the day were keeping me from slipping easefully into sleep. I must say that, even though Continental Europe has little else to recommend it, I cannot fault in any way the excellent and comprehensive training they give their *au pairs*.

I heard Francesca's soft knock at the door and let her in.

"Good morning, dear Francesca."

"Good morning, Sir Errol," she purred in her charming accent. I'd asked her on numerous occasions to dispense with the "Sir" but she persisted, saying she enjoyed hearing the words come out her mouth. To work her way up from humble *au pair* to the exalted task of serving a knight was a leap few women could dream of. If it gave her pleasure to address me as "Sir," so be it.

She poured me a cup of her fine coffee, stirred in the teaspoon of cream I require and awaited my approval.

I took my first sip and savored the life-giving infusion of the dark richness. I rolled it around my mouth and let it slide down my throat.

"Ah. Perfection once again," I said to Francesca.

Her long eyelashes fluttered in delight. "Is there anything else I can do for you while I'm here, Sir Errol? May I run you a bath or lay your clothes out for you?"

"I'm feeling quite well bathed from last night," I said, "but I could certainly use a little help on the clothing side."

"Will this be an active day for you, Sir Errol, or should we dress you for lounging here at home?"

"Active, very active. I must careen out into the suburbs on the train and then join friends at the club for a vigorous round of billiards."

"Then how about your camel-hair blazer and your plus-fours? Add a pair of argyle socks and you'll be both nattily attired and suited up for the rigors of travel."

"I think the plus-fours and argyle might be a bit too natty for a Sunday," I said. "We don't wish to cause alarm to churchgoers. In the spirit of adventure I'll wear the argyle socks, but let's at least cover them with long trousers."

"Of course, Sir Errol. I wasn't thinking."

"You're forgiven, dear. We English take a more somber approach to our religious activities than do the frenzied worshippers of your native Tuscany, given as they are to wild displays of passion brought on by heady incense and the constant clanging of bells."

"I've noticed, Sir Errol, that you do not seem to take part in these somber religious gatherings of which you speak."

"Sadly, no," I said. "A few of my step-mothers gave it a try with me but it never took hold. My main objection was that it seemed excessive to have Ten Commandments, that number being far too many for the average person to keep in mind. It was my feeling then and now that two or three really solid commandments would do just fine. In any case, I elected to make up my own commandments as I go along. It simplifies things marvelously."

I had stronger opinions on the subject of religion but I didn't want to burden Francesca's tender young mind with them. In my view, human beings understand God about as well as our pet goldfish understand us. It had always seemed to me the height of arrogance for us humans to prattle on about God when most of us can't even treat our household staff decently.

Lady Forsythia had even gone so far as to ask me not to proclaim some of my opinions in public, following an incident at a dinner party at which she felt I went a bit overboard. I had merely stated that anyone claiming to know to know anything about God ought to be confined to a zoo and taunted mercilessly until they surrendered the notion. In her view, my utterance of this opinion was a causative factor in our being asked to leave the premises. In my defense, it must be said that Lady Forsythia does not handle embarrassment well.

Francesca said, "Sometimes, Sir Errol, I have difficulty knowing when you are serious and when you are not."

"It's safest if you always assume the latter, my dear."

She laid out my clothing for me then bid me farewell to go back down to her studies. I had helped her set up a course of instruction that would lead to a certificate as a legal secretary. There was always a shortage of people in that profession, thanks to our countrymen's increasing zeal for suing each other. I had no doubt Francesca would gain employment in a good law firm. I was of course worried that it might harm her character and innate sense of morality to be situated amongst a bunch of barristers, but given her broad range of skills, her beauty and her keen eye for career advancement, it was also entirely possible that Francesca would be pursued to matrimony by some rich, be-wigged QC and end up presiding over a manse of her own.

The day was bright and crisp but I took along my bumbershoot, just in case the fickle English weather had its cunning way with me. It was my intention to hike across Hyde Park to Paddington Station, thus putting a mile or two on my legs before boarding the express train out to the shire of Oxford. I was counting on a brisk half-hour in the rain-cleansed air to set me straight regarding the penetrating questions Helga had needled me with last evening. It was Grandmother Hyde's firm opinion that there were few human problems that couldn't be cured by a good, brisk walk. I aimed to give my legs a stretch and do some serious grappling with the conundrum that Helga had implanted in my mind.

The park was already thronged with Londoners out to enjoy the unexpected grace of fine sunshine. Being Hyde Park, it was also thronged with every sort of hawker, from wisecracking fishmongers crying out "Fresh oysters! Fresh cockles!" to earnest members of obscure religions passing out poorly printed pamphlets. Passing a young woman selling crumpets, apparently of her own manufacture, my salivary glands leapt into action, reminding me that I had somehow managed to get through the whole morning so far fueled only by Francesca's coffee.

As I strode across the sun-bathed park the idea sprang to mind of visiting a bakery café I liked just on the other side, run by a Frenchman who had a way with croissants, especially those of the almond variety. On previous visits I had found the combination of crunchy exterior and gooey interior to be utterly irresistible. So caught up was I in thoughts of these marvelous pastries that I got all the way across the park without ever doing any of the philosophical musings I had planned. Damn those French! Their superb baked goods are the mortal enemies of deep reflection.

I came out of the park onto Bayswater Road and made a beeline for Café du Georges, where I was agreeably served with my almond croissant and a *café au lait.* Thus fortified, I legged it onward to Paddington, intending to occupy myself during my train journey by giving life's deeper questions a good, solid pondering. However, after getting settled on the train I had just begun to ponder when the rhythmic clacking of the train wheels on the track lulled me into a torpor that turned into a pleasant little snooze. I awoke just as the train was pulling into the Oxford station, my hair slightly mussed but otherwise in fine fettle.

The weather was still fine when I got off the train, but even in the best of weather I didn't fancy walking the eight miles or so out to Blenheim. Also, I didn't know my way around very well. Like any Cambridge man worth his salt, I'd always avoided the environs of Oxford. I didn't want to clatter around in a carriage or one of the new motorized taxis, a bit of stealth being required for the task at hand.

I was casting about for a solution when I spotted a bicycle shop just up the street. A sign in the window proudly proclaimed that they offered Royal Enfield bicycles, the very brand I owned, now reposing for the winter in the basement of my building. This fine machine, equipped with the new hand-operated brakes, had borne me on many jaunts around the city.

I slapped down a pound's deposit and was soon rolling along at a merry pace out toward Blenheim. It was certainly chillier than one would have liked a bicycle ride to be, but it also felt quite exhilarating to be riding again. To me, the bicycle had always seemed the ideal form of transportation, especially compared to the loathsome horse and the noisy, smoke-belching automobiles that were taking over the roads. With bicycles you pedal along under your own power and don't have to clean up after them.

I was pleased that each year brought more innovations that made riding easier and more fun. Rumor had it that the Royal Enfield people were about to launch a new machine with a brake on the rear wheel as well as the front, plus the newly invented 3-speed gear-shifting mechanism some fellows named Sturmey and Archer had sharked up out in Nottingham.

(If, Dear Reader, you are beginning to suspect that I am something of an enthusiast when it comes to bicycles, you are correct. While I was certain I had my detractors for my cycling passions—some people are terminally allergic to fun in any form—I'm equally certain that those pickers of nit had never felt the zestful pleasures of zipping along at a decent clip with the fresh air streaming through their hair.)

As I pedaled along on that fine, brisk morning, I began to think that perhaps the feeling of exhilaration coursing through me was sufficient to serve as the life purpose Helga was goading me to discover. What's wrong with just following one's enthusiasms through life? Do we all need to be running off to discover some horrid new river in Borneo or grinding away in the laboratory finding a cure for some dread disease? I made a mental note to try out this new theory of mine on Helga at my earliest opportunity.

I was so caught up in the back-and-forth going on between my ears that I shot right past the turnoff for Blenheim. I screeched to a halt and pedaled back around onto the road to the palace, which I could see looming in the distance. According to my cab-driving informant, Charlie, the house I was looking for was tucked in a wood within a stone's throw of the palace grounds. According to Charlie's instructions I would find a dirt road to the house just beyond the western edge of the palace's property.

Charlie turned out to be true to his word. When I pedaled around to the western side of the palace I saw the low rock wall that marked the outer edge of the grounds, and sure enough, there was a dirt road that led into a stand of woods. I rode over and tucked my bicycle behind some trees.

I set off on foot down the road and within a quarter-mile saw the house in the distance. I paused and gave it a look-over. It was a one-story affair that had probably been a crofter's cottage before somebody added onto it. Charlie had described it as a "bunker," and as I surveyed it I understood what he meant. The original stone cottage was flanked by two wings, which looked like they had been added on later with a different type of rock. Set back from the road and surrounded by forest, the house couldn't possibly get much sunlight even on the finest day. All in all, it was a singularly creepy-looking place.

My throat suddenly felt dry, and I realized I had cold tickles of fear playing around my innards. My hand involuntarily felt for the comfort of the little single-shot Derringer I was carrying in the right-hand pocket of my jacket. I stepped behind a tree and leaned up against it for a moment to get myself sorted out. I hadn't felt a wave of fear surge through my belly since the sad affair of the tiger and the Belgian countess half a year ago.

I took a few big breaths to chase the fear out of my body and began stealing closer to the house, staying behind the trees across the road from it. When I was directly in front of it I peered out from behind the trees again; from this angle I could see smoke coming out of the chimney. It looked at least like somebody was home.

How right I was.

A moment later my ears perceived a rattling sound from the direction I'd just come, and into my left field of vision came a man in work clothing pushing my bicycle along the dirt road. Just as I was getting my astonishment under control I heard a voice boom out, "Come in, Sir Errol. I've been expecting you!"

A man was standing at the front door of the cottage, beckoning me to come over.

In my amazement I stumbled out from the cover of the trees and approached the cottage. The man was a thin, scholarly-looking fellow with wire-rimmed glasses, dressed in a well-made grey suit and wearing a purple ascot instead of a tie.

"I had my man, Travers, fetch your bicycle," he said, speaking in a proper English accent with just a trace of Scottish burr left on it. "I wanted to make sure it didn't get purloined by any of the miscreants that are forever prowling our woods." His sly smile let me know he was referring to me as one of those miscreants.

I came up the steps and shook his proffered hand. "I'm Errol Hyde, as you already appear to know."

He said, "Yes, of course, Sir Errol. I have been quietly following your career for quite some time now."

"You have?"

"Indeed. I'm everywhere. Am I not Professor Moriarty, the great organizing principle of London crime?"

My mind froze. "You're Moriarty?"

He roared with laughter. "No, my dear Mr. Hyde, I'm merely tugging your leg, as the Americans say. I'm afraid Professor Moriarty is a figment of Holmes's fevered imagination, which he goes far out of his way to stoke with all manner of stimulants. My name is Malcolm Stewart and I would be pleased to have you come in for a visit."

The interior was neat as a pin, almost sterile in its cleanliness and lack of clutter. He gestured toward a plain wooden table with nothing on it but a pad of paper and an inkwell. There were two austere, straight-back chairs at the table; he pulled one out for me and invited me to take a seat.

He said, "I believe you prefer coffee to tea, do you not, Sir Errol?"

"Indeed I do, and how would you know such a thing?"

He gave me his sly smile again. "All will be revealed in the fullness of time, but for now, would you say 'Yes' to a cup?"

"I have never knowingly turned one down, Mr. Stewart, providing it is made with care and high-quality ingredients."

"I think you will approve of the ingredients. If I am not mistaken, you favor the rich, earthy bean of Indonesia, preferably from the island of Sumatra."

"Good grief, man, have you been peeking through the window of my kitchen?"

"Not quite, Sir Errol, but my sources tell me you have been observed on many occasions buying that particular type of bean from the fine establishment of Fortnum and Mason." He gestured to a glass jar of the dark, glistening beans. "I purchased a pound of Sumatra beans from Fortnum's just this week. According to the clerk, these are the very beans you favor."

In a former and more civilized time one would have a clerk flogged for that kind of impertinent gossip, but he was not wrong. I do love a good Indonesian bean.

My host tamped down the grounds into the paper cone and poured an ounce or so of water into them. "It's a trick I learned from my mother, Sir Errol. My father always said she made the finest cup of coffee in the world. Her secret was to dash a little water over the grounds first, in order to remove bitterness from them." He dumped out the small amount of coffee that had dripped through the beans and proceeded to pour the rest of the water over them.

"Would you like a drop of cream?"

I felt reassured that he seemed not to know I indeed enjoyed a tiny splash of cream in my coffee. Perhaps there were a few things about my daily affairs of which he was unaware. "Yes, one teaspoonful of cream would be ideal." I tipped the little pitcher and watched the cream turn the coffee into my preferred shade, a chocolate brown.

Mr. Stewart watched me carefully, waiting for me to take a sip.

I took my first sip and felt my eyes widen involuntarily. By God it was extraordinary! It was rich and deep and rolled across the tongue without a trace of bitterness. I could taste the darkness of the Sumatran forest in its depths, the overtones redolent with tropical spice. I saw what appeared to be a genuine smile break out on my host's face.

"Sir Errol, your very expression has made me a happy man!" He took a sip from his own cup and smiled with approval. "Shall we take our cups back to the table? Now that we are well fortified I should like to describe a matter of some importance to me, and perhaps gain your assistance in resolving it. I shall also happily answer all the questions I'm sure you have, such as the primary one, 'What's this all about, anyway?' "

When we had situated ourselves again in the front room, Stewart put his hands on his knees and leaned forward to fix me intently with his eyes. "First, let me explain why I have gone to such arcane lengths to get you here, Sir Errol. I make my living as a freelance consultant. People consult me for many types of problems and enterprises, some of which are not strictly legal. I take you into my confidence because you strike me as the sort of gentleman who is not bound by the social strictures that so limit the thinking of the average citizen."

"I do not involve myself in anything that might be considered dishonorable."

"Nor do I, but first let's calibrate what we both consider dishonorable. If a tyrant is abusing a wife or a nation, I believe it is honorable to eliminate him. I ask you sincerely, Sir Errol: Wouldn't you agree?"

"I would agree without reservation. Have you eliminated any tyrants recently? I could name you a few whom I might nominate."

"I have indeed, but not ones whose names you might recognize."

"Well, then, perhaps you could give me an example."

"Certainly. I recently assisted in the permanent removal of a respectable Swiss banker who was behaving in a most un-respectable manner at home. His two older daughters and the mother consulted me about the father's disgusting sexual proclivities. The two older daughters, having been victimized by this creature I hesitate to call a "father," were now frantic with concern that his perverted eye was falling upon their two younger sisters. They wished, above all else, for the two tender young ladies not to be corrupted by this despicable man. They also wanted to do everything possible to keep the family's name from being besmirched by the taint of scandal."

"They asked you to kill him?"

"No, of course not. They simply presented me with the problem and I devised a solution without burdening them with the details of my plan."

"Are you at liberties to tell me what outcome you obtained?"

"Certainly. Some months later he suffered a cardiac incident at work. He was in the habit of having a glass of his favorite whiskey each day at close of business. One day he collapsed with glass in hand, an unfortunate victim of heart failure, so sad in a man of such robust health. He was treated to a grand funeral, with many testimonials to his character intoned by solid, Swiss burghers. The widow's grief was mollified somewhat by inheritance of the estate and a large sum of insurance money. She is now raising her girls in a sunny clime."

"No doubt an operative in your employ visited the banker on the day of his demise, perhaps to add a new dimension of flavor to the favored whiskey."

"You have a devious mind, Sir Errol, a quality I prize highly in a man. And your perception of the activities that led to this awful man's death is accurate in the main. The late banker had also been quite abusive to his underlings at the bank, making it no trouble at all to persuade his secretary to express her long-held resentment by attending to the whiskey. I believe she is also now taking her ease in the balmy tropics."

"I'm curious as to how one gets into your line of work," I said.

"I'd be equally curious to know how the Seventh Earl Of Hyde Manor got into the private detective game, but I'm sure you'll tell me some day if it pleases you. To give immediate satisfaction to your curiosity, though, I got into my unusual pursuit by rising to the rank of major in His Majesty's armed forces. I was never one for marching about with rifles and sabers, so I spent my career in the obscure but essential field of 'procurement.' My job was to get whatever my higher-ups needed, from boots for new recruits to after-dinner cognac for the generals to imbibe."

"And from there you graduated to freelance procurement, or so I would suppose."

"Indeed. Once one learns the art of doing favors for people, a world of employment opportunities open up."

"Odd you should say that, because it was through the doing of a favor that I first discovered a fondness for detection. I'll perhaps tell you on another occasion, but first, why didn't you just call on me? Why go to all the trouble to lure me out here?"

"I confess a weakness for amusing myself. That flaw in my character is largely to blame. I suspect you can sympathize."

"Yes, although I do not regard my sincere dedication to amusing myself as any kind of flaw. Rather I think of it as an art form and a pinnacle achievement of the whole human experiment."

"I like your attitude better, Sir Errol, and will immediately adopt it as my own."

Wise fellow! "Tell me this, Mr. Stewart—at what point did you intervene in the prince's misadventure?"

"He consulted me about the matter of the chambermaid before contacting you. He was considering asking either Holmes or you to assist him. It was I who suggested that he talk to you rather than Holmes."

"Why didn't you offer to help him yourself?"

"I was on my way to Switzerland, tying up some loose ends in the affair of the banker."

"Why the mask?"

"What mask?"

"The two brothers said they were brought here by horse-drawn carriage and given their assignment to beat up the butler by a man and a woman in masks."

His brow creased. "What on earth are you saying? They came here to this house?" He sounded as confused as I was.

I tried to explain what the Bulgarian brothers had told me.

He put on an expression of utmost sincerity. "I just returned from Switzerland three days ago. I know nothing about any masked man or woman."

From his bewildered expression I deduced that he was telling the truth. "Perhaps an elaborate joke was played upon you in your absence. Could it be that the masked people borrowed your house for the occasion while you were away?"

He rubbed his chin thoughtfully. "I did notice a few things out of place when I returned. My man Travers was off visiting his aged mother in York while I was abroad, so perhaps my premises were indeed occupied under false pretenses. My niece was also staying here while I was away, so there may be another explanation."

"Your niece?"

"Yes, dear Freda. She is the daughter of my late, beloved sister, Wilhelmina, who was married to a Slovenian businessman. Freda has spent most of her life abroad until her mother's death last year. My aim is to help Freda get a new life started here in London. Her father, while hugely successful, is not a suitable role model for many reasons, not the least of which is that he is a thief, smuggler and all-around scoundrel."

"I see. Where is Freda now? I should like to meet her and ask her if she knows anything about the masked couple." A vague picture was beginning to form in my mind.

"I'm sure she'd love to meet you. She said she was going to read and take a nap in her bedroom. Let me see if she's up and around."

He left the room and came back a few moments later. "She'll be out in just a moment. Would you like another cup of coffee while we wait?"

"Dear fellow, your coffee is so rich and delicious that you need never again ask if I would like a cup. Just assume that I do and always will."

He dipped his head in a slight bow. "Your approval does me great honor, Sir Errol. As you can no doubt tell, my coffee-making prowess is a modest source of pride to me." He headed out to the kitchen to refill my cup.

Almost the moment he left the room I heard another door open. Into the room strode a young woman of remarkable beauty who favored me with a big, knowing smile. She was wearing a fashionable skirt and blouse, with a red silk scarf tossed casually around her neck. So great was my astonishment that I was unable to find words for a moment.

"Hello again, Sir Errol. This time you may call me Freda."

It was Ariana, chambermaid and charmer of princes.

CHAPTER SEVEN

My jaw was still hanging slack a moment later when Stewart came back into the room. He was chuckling so vigorously the cups in his hands were rattling on their saucers. "Oh, the look on your face, Sir Errol! I would give anything to have a photograph of it! You must forgive me—I fancy myself something of a trickster!"

There's nothing better than a good practical joke, except of course when it's played on oneself. I felt a rise of umbrage, indignant that this Malcolm fellow was having me on.

He set the coffee down on the table. "I note the look of astonishment on your face has tightened into irritation. Please don't be angry, Sir Errol. I already confessed my weakness for self-amusement."

I did my best to get my composure back. I said, "How much of this whole business is artifice, Stewart? Is Freda really your niece?"

This made both of them laugh. "Happily she is not," Stewart said. "She is from Slovenia and her father is a first-class scoundrel—that much is true. I happen to know he is a scoundrel because I have employed some of his nefarious skills in my own schemes. But in the area of nieces and nephews I have been left completely bereft: I am an only child and have no family left on earth, quite like yourself. Freda serves both as my domestic companion and as my trusted cohort in many of the projects I undertake. Now, please, let's sit together and enjoy our coffee. I believe I can compensate you for my indulgence in sophomoric humor by giving you two splendidly interesting problems to solve."

I could hear heavy splats of rain beginning to fall on the roof, signifying that the fine day I had pedaled out in was rapidly deteriorating.

Having no wish to go out into the wetness and chill, I overcame my irritation at his pranks and sat down to hear what he had to say.

"First off, we'd like your help in persuading the prince that his love would best be requited elsewhere than with the imaginary woman named Ariana. I am not a jealous man, but I am rather a practical one. It serves no one to have a prince moping about the palace thinking his great love has run out on him. Let's find a way to set him down easily."

"I take it that whatever purpose was intended by the arrangement has been fulfilled. What *was* the purpose, anyway?"

"It was simply an information-gathering pursuit. When I heard Kudlow was hiring staff for the prince my ears perked up; I thought perhaps some benefit could be made of having a person on the inside. My work depends upon having information before other people know it. Freda's attentions to the prince produced a gold mine of useful nuggets."

I felt myself bristling somewhat about the meretricious aspects of the arrangement. I even began to feel a tad of compassion for the prince. The poor fellow never knew what hit him.

As if reading my mind, Stewart said, "I see by the look on your face that you disapprove of some of my tactics. It grieves me to confess that a deep and unredeemable amoral streak runs through me. I've come to peace with it, and I would hope that you could find it in your heart to do the same. However, I promise you I will never ask you to do anything you would consider dishonorable."

Such a straightforward appeal resonated with me; I asked him to continue.

"You have known the prince a great deal longer than I have. Would you be willing to devise a plan for bringing his romance with Ariana to a close in a way that doesn't wound the poor fellow's feelings?"

It seemed a reasonable request so I said, "Yes. Let me think about the best way to do that. In the meantime, perhaps you could satisfy a curiosity of mine that, while crass, leaps nimbly to the forefront of my mind: what's in it for me?"

"I was coming to that, Sir Errol. What I can offer you is the opportunity to change the course of human history."

"Oh, just that? How is counseling a lovesick prince going to accomplish that noble goal? And how can we know if we go about changing history we're going to nudge it in the right direction?"

"All excellent questions, my good man, and to answer them I must begin with a question of my own. Do you have much experience with spiritualism?"

I couldn't prevent a slight groan from escaping my lips. "I have heard that spiritualism is going through another surge of popularity among the intelligentsia, but I cannot profess to be any sort of expert in the matter. I attended a séance some years ago but found it to be utter rubbish."

"Quite so," he said. "Most of it is fraud pure and simple, designed to prey on lonely, grief-stricken people in order to separate them from their money. Very occasionally, however, you find a genuine diamond among the rhinestones."

"And you have found such a diamond? Someone who can actually predict the future?"

"We have."

"Well, then, why don't you turn him loose on the stock market or take him to Monte Carlo for the roulette?"

"First of all, he is a she."

"Well, whoever it is, if she's any good at all she should be able to predict a simple thing such as whether the ball will land on red or black. A few spins of the wheel and you would certainly be able to afford much grander lodgings than this."

"It doesn't work that way."

"I thought not."

"Don't be so insufferably smug, Sir Errol."

"Steady on, Mr. Stewart. Don't be so quick to condemn insufferable smugness. You have no idea how many generations it takes to cultivate that sort of attitude."

"I can barely imagine. And for the record, Sir Errol, I merely rent this house for a strategic purpose. My actual dwelling is in Mayfair."

"My apologies for belittling your abode—it was unseemly of me. However, if this psychic of yours can't pick ponies or spot winners in the stock market, what good is she?"

"I shall side-step your sarcasm and answer your question quite specifically. The lady in question can see the future course of history."

"Ah, then. No good at roulette but a whiz when it comes to the future of the human race."

Freda said, "Please, Sir Errol. Just listen." She leaned forward and put her hand on my thigh, causing a wave of delicious energy to course through my nether regions. The animal magnetism of the young woman was undeniable; I would have happily listened to her read aloud the dreadfully dreary essays of William Hazlitt if she would keep her hand on my thigh like that.

Stewart said, "I welcome your skepticism, Sir Errol. I even celebrate it. You are widely known for your discerning mind, but in this case I also request that you approach this subject with an open heart."

"It is an unusual request, but I shall do what I can to honor it. Please go on."

Just then I heard the clattering of a horse-drawn carriage outside the cottage.

"Ah, I believe our other guest has arrived," Stewart said. "Excuse me for a moment while I attend to her."

Freda still had her hand on my thigh. She leaned forward and said, "Please be patient, Sir Errol. I promise you won't be disappointed."

Moments later Stewart returned, ushering before him a tiny, stout woman who wore a black mask and a scarlet hooded cloak.

From the wisps of hair that stuck out from under the hood I could see it was a blazing reddish-orange color that nature typically reserves for carrots.

"Sir Errol, I present to you Madame Cynthia DeLoach, or Madame C as we like to call her. Madame C, this is the esteemed private detective and knight of the realm, Sir Errol Hyde."

I bowed to her and she returned a slight bow in my direction. She made no attempt to remove the mask. Stewart helped her off with her cloak, revealing a well-made black velvet dress and a mane of hair tied in back with a red ribbon.

I have a firm policy of not lying unless absolutely necessary, so it was difficult for me to utter the required response of "Pleased to meet you." I wasn't sure if I was pleased to meet her or not, since I couldn't see whom I was meeting.

She intuited my hesitation correctly. "Do you find my mask off-putting, Sir Errol?" She spoke in an unexpectedly deep, husky voice for such a small woman. I had trouble discerning her accent; it was proper English but had a slight lilt to it. Welsh?

Her question caught me off guard with its boldness, but I managed to stutter out something bordering on an honest response. "Yes, I suppose I do."

"Some people find my face even more off-putting," she said, taking off the mask to reveal a sweet, round face of perhaps sixty years of age. Then I noticed what was obviously the reason for her mask: a red streak of a scar across her left cheek. She pointed to the scar and said, "A parting gift from an ex-husband."

"I'm so sorry," I said.

She dismissed my comment with a curt shake of her head. "It was my doing. I chose the wrong moment to inform him I was leaving him for another man. He was in mid-smear with a butter knife and lost his composure. Fortunately for me, we had not yet come to the rib roast when he would have been armed with a sharper knife."

Stewart said, "Let's sit down, shall we?"

"I smell fresh coffee," Madame C said. "I want some." Stewart dashed off to the kitchen to fetch a cup for her.

She was definitely a woman who spoke her mind. I had only been in her presence a couple of minutes but I already knew a great deal more about her than I knew about some of my longtime acquaintances.

She wasn't finished, either. "If you're wondering what happened to the knife-wielding ex-husband, karma caught up with him a few months later: they found him face-down in a mud puddle outside a Brixton gaming club, the apparent victim of brigands."

"A fitting end," Freda said.

"No good can ever come of visiting Brixton,"

I offered helpfully.

Stewart returned with her coffee. She gave him a nod of thanks and took a sip, followed by a sigh of approval. Then abruptly she spun to face me and said, "Now, young man, let's see if we can give you something to live for."

"Beg pardon?"

"You know what I mean, Sir Errol. You know quite well that your existence is devoid of deeper meaning. You also know that you have a deep hunger to do something more with your life than indulge your petty enthusiasms."

My mind spun into a whirl. Just an hour or two ago I had been mounting a case that my enthusiasms were sufficient to serve as a life purpose. Now here I was, locked in the gaze of a pair of exceptionally piercing green eyes, getting lectured on the subject by a tiny lady with an imperious manner and an untidy relationship history. I was tempted to call attention to the gall with which I was being treated, but at the same time something inside compelled me to keep listening.

"Would you agree with me, Sir Errol? Or am I just talking into the wind here?"

I started to defend my position but I couldn't muster the necessary indignation. Eventually I found words and said, "I would cautiously agree."

"Ah, he would CAUTIOUSLY agree!" she said with a chuckle. "And what do you base your caution upon, Sir Errol?"

She had me there. I leapt into the unknown and said, "I believe I am trying to preserve aspects of myself that have in the past enabled me to survive and even thrive in times of duress."

"Good thinking, Sir Errol. Let me elaborate on that idea with a bit of wisdom you will no doubt discover in good time. The very parts of you that make you successful in the first half of life are the very barriers you must overcome to be successful in the second half. If I perceive your age correctly, you are around forty, are you not?"

"You are correct. In a few months I will embark upon that new decade."

"Then let me tell you bluntly. If you want to make yourself miserable indeed, try to preserve that precious ego of yours as you proceed into your forties and fifties. The forces of the universe will conspire to batter you mercilessly the more you cling to it. Your only freedom after the age of forty comes from shedding your ego, not bolstering it." She folded her hands in her lap and fixed me again with those blazing green eyes of hers.

I couldn't think of what to say to all that. Under normal circumstances I didn't spend a great deal of time cogitating about the forces of the universe, but here was this little woman going on about it with a degree of certitude that both alarmed and fascinated me.

She wasn't finished yet. "Malcolm regales me with tales of your brilliance as a detective, but tell me this: isn't it crucial for a detective to let go of pre-conceived notions in favor of letting the evidence guide you?"

"Indeed it is."

"Then I am merely suggesting you apply that same wisdom to yourself."

It pained me somewhat to admit it, but I was beginning to think there might be some value in what the woman was saying. Why not give her a listen?

"All right," I said. "I will set aside for the moment my rampant skepticism and invite you to enlighten me."

She gave a curt nod. "A wise move indeed, Sir Errol. Now listen carefully. A great stirring is coming to Europe, an agitation that will eventually cause the whole world to tremble in its wake. Can you feel those tremors coming, Sir Errol?"

I dare say one didn't need to be a psychic to predict that sort of thing. Europe was forever getting stirred up about one thing or the other. In fact, there seemed to be some sort of big agitation every twenty or thirty years. I had often wondered if humanity had some kind of allergy to peace.

"I confess I cannot. I read the newspapers, so I know that wars are always springing up here and there, but I don't see how that might concern an Englishman."

"The conflagration of which I speak will without question concern Englishmen. I have seen images of thousands of our countrymen being slaughtered in a single day."

It sounded far-fetched to me. "The citizens of the Continent seem no more riled up than usual, Madame C. In fact, they seem to have been behaving in a fairly civilized manner for quite a few years now, given their heritage and proclivities. Even the French have tempered their enthusiasm for publicly beheading their kings and queens. This is 1908. How far in the future do you see this great conflagration to be?"

She shook her head. "When I am in the spirit world, where I see these images, I have only the vaguest sense of ordinary time. However, it feels close, not decades or centuries but mere years."

That's the problem with psychics and séances and such: they're always speaking to dead people and making grand predictions, but where's the proof? Maybe I'll believe in spiritualism if a psychic can connect me with the departed former owner of my home, especially if he can be induced to tell me the location of the spare set of keys I was promised just a day before his unfortunate collision with a runaway milk lorry. All turned out well—I got the building for a song from the poor fellow's heirs—but the missing keys continued to rankle. Death is no excuse to skip out on one's obligations.

However, I had promised to keep my mind and heart open at least a crack, so I put aside my urge to make a few more skeptical remarks. I said, "Please tell me more."

Stewart was getting quite lathered up as he listened to her. He was practically squirming in his seat, and "niece" Freda had a rapt expression on her face as well. Even though they had probably heard it all before, they couldn't seem to get enough of Madame C.

"I shall," she said, "and if there were ever a moment for you to listen with your keenest attention, this would be it." She paused and locked me in her eye-beams. "Are you listening with all your faculties, Sir Errol?"

This seemed a bit overly dramatic to me, but I went along with it. "I believe I am, Madame C, with the caveat that none of can ever know for certain whether we are in touch with all our faculties."

"Very clever, Sir Errol. Now put your cleverness aside and listen to me."

Damn the woman's cheek! Part of me felt like chucking the whole affair and telling her she could keep her precious information. Get somebody else to change the course of world history! However, I managed to stifle my pique and told her to go on.

"Even though my gifts do not allow me to be specific about time, they do allow me to see some people and places in clear detail."

Stewart said, "That's why we're here in Blenheim."

Madame C said, "That's correct. I had a clear vision that a momentous event would occur in the environs of Blenheim, an event that must not be interrupted. I saw that a great knave would try to prevent this event from happening, with dire consequences for our beloved land."

"But if I understand you correctly, you do not have any idea when this momentous event is likely to happen."

"Again, it feels close in time, but you are correct. I cannot see for certain. However, I do get the sense that the consequences of the event will stretch many decades into the future, well beyond our own lifetimes."

Her story was beginning to sound more and more like one of those old Dickens novels, all about the best of times and the worst of times. Now the story had even sprouted an evil villain. I said, "Tell me more of this great knave of whom you speak."

"Ah, yes—the chess master."

This was getting better and better. "Yes, of course, the chess master."

"You are mocking me, Sir Errol. I'm told the sharp-tipped rapier of your wit is much admired in fashionable London."

I admitted I had something of a reputation for turning a humorous phrase.

She said, "Well, here that is of absolutely no value."

Ouch! Caned again. "My apologies, Madame C. On many days my rapier-like wit, as you describe it, wakes up before I do. Please tell me more about this chess-master."

"In one of my visions I saw a man in a mountain hideaway, moving pieces on a chess board. He would place them, stare at them for a while, and then move them into another pattern. In another vision I saw him present at a great house fire, and in another he was at a large political gathering of some sort."

"What did this man look like?"

"Hairless of face and head, pale in color, very tall."

"And in your vision, what was this hairless chess master really up to?"

"Creating maximum chaos and hatred, the two emotions at the center of his soul."

"Goodness! He sounds like the very Devil the religious folks are always going on about."

"I'm afraid he's much worse than any Devil they can manufacture in their fevered minds."

"Really! How can that be? I thought their imaginations were doing a pretty good job of it, with the horns and all."

"Precisely the point, Sir Errol. He is worse because he's completely ordinary—absolutely, utterly ordinary. You could pass by him on the street and never know what nefarious plot occupies his mind. As your beloved Shakespeare says, the Prince Of Darkness is always a gentleman."

"You almost sound as if you know this man."

"I visit him often in my visions. I want to know everything I can about him."

"So that . . . ?"

"So that love and harmony can replace chaos and hatred in our world."

"That might take a while."

"It might, Sir Errol, but I am a patient woman. Think of eternity as ripples spreading across a pond, set in motion by a pebble dropped by our shy, mysterious Creator. Our little lives are the ripple passing through us. What we do in that little life of ours affects the ripples going forward through time. I am simply trying to add harmony as the ripple passes through me."

I wasn't quite sure where she was going with all this business about eternity and pond-ripples, so I tried to steer her back to the practical side of things. "What do you see as my role in this eternal drama? Do you have a specific task you would have me engage in?"

Stewart jumped in with an excited "Yes!"

"Please tell me."

He leaned forward and gripped me with his eyes. "We would like you to employ your genius for detection in a very practical way.

In her visions Madame C managed to see details about three of the moves."

"Beg pardon?"

She said, "I caught a brief look at three of the chess moves. One was a political meeting of some sort, the second a house fire in the countryside, and the third was the potential murder of two young lovers here in Blenheim. The ordinary Devil of whom we speak was present at each of those events."

"And these events have not yet taken place?"

"Correct, but in my vision they feel imminent."

"Let me make sure I understand what you're asking. First, you want me to solve three crimes that haven't happened yet. Second, you do not know the identities of the perpetrators, the supposed victims of these crimes or when they are to take place. Third, the architect of all this—the one I must find and defeat—is unknown to you here in the material world. Is that about right?"

Her eyes blazed at me. "Yes, but please do not mock me! It is essential that we intervene! In my vision I saw a connection between the house fire, the political gathering and the young lovers. I do not know the significance; I could only see the line of energy connecting the events. If we can understand this connection we can prevent the murder."

"And thus change the course of human history in a positive direction," I said.

"Are you mocking me again, Sir Errol?"

"I am trying not to, but the temptation has a constant grip on me."

I didn't know what to make of her "line of energy" malarkey but there was no doubt about her passion. Color infused her face, making more vivid the slash of scar across her left cheek.

I said, "If I understand correctly, you have no more information—no "clues" as the detective stories are wont to say—that can point me in a fruitful direction."

"I think I've told you everything, but you're welcome to interrogate me to help me uncover details perhaps forgotten."

"I would definitely want to do that, Madame C, should I take the case, but there is a much more fundamental problem: I don't think I'm the man for the job. There's nothing solid for me to go on, and with all due respect, there is much here for the skeptical part of my mind to feast upon. Surely, you must entertain the possibility that these visions of yours are simply figments of your rich imagination."

"Certainly I have, Sir Errol. I'm not a dolt. All I can tell you is that my visions have a different feeling about them than my ordinary fantasies. They are as different from each other as day is to night."

"Still," I said, "the mind has a way of playing tricks on us all."

She sighed. "So you will not help us, Sir Errol?"

"I'm afraid not. The whole affair is too flimsy for me to get a grasp on. I fear I would be chasing shadows around. Solving real crimes is difficult enough, but when they are being perpetrated from the spirit world, if such a world exists, the problems become impenetrable. Now, I think it is time for me to thank you for your hospitality and make my way back home." I stood up and began to gather my things.

She closed her eyes and leaned back in her chair. "Very well. Before you go, though, I have a message to you from your mother."

"I beg your pardon?"

"You heard me. I bring you a message from your mother. Would you like to hear it?"

My mind scrambled for a suitable response. Part of me felt outraged at being the butt of a psychic parlor trick, but another part of me wanted to find out what she was getting at. Finally I just said, "All right."

"She wants you to know it had nothing to do with you."

"What had nothing to do with me?"

"You know what I'm talking about, Sir Errol. She wants you to know that her departure and subsequent suicide had nothing at all to do with you personally."

That flummoxed me. "Nonsense! Of course it had to do with me. I was the one it happened to."

"That's just the point. It would have happened to any child who happened to be there. She didn't want to be a mother. It wasn't about you personally. She would have felt that way about any child."

Dear Reader, I confess that her words hit me like a hard rap on the noggin. As a child I had sometimes found myself musing in bitter wonderment about that very issue: what did my mother find so revolting about me that it drove her to bolt from the family home? Later, after I had more opportunity to observe my father's beastly behavior with my various stepmothers, I realized it probably wasn't totally my fault. Somehow, though, it had always rankled me that she had departed so quickly after my birth. Now this tiny lady was telling me I needn't take the whole thing personally, and, *mirabile dictu*, she was absolutely right. Mother hadn't left *me* behind; she would have left *any* kid behind.

Madame C said, "This idea appears to bring relief to your face, Sir Errol."

I stammered out a thank-you and sat back down. My skeptical mind broke through and I asked her, "How did you know my mother committed suicide? Did you gain that information from the spirit world?"

She shook her head. "No, Malcolm told me."

Stewart said, "I've researched you very carefully, my friend, just as I would do for anyone I'm considering working with."

Ha! I thought as much. "And what about that business of 'Don't take it personally.' Where did you get that bit from?' "

She gave me a smile that looked sympathetic. "See what you are doing, Sir Errol? You had a moment of feeling your passions genuinely stirred by what I said, and then your critical mind kicked back in. Now you are feeling querulous. I recommend you stop doing that to yourself at your earliest opportunity. Let your passions be stirred, Sir Errol! I promise it won't kill you."

I could feel the truth of what she was saying but she still had not answered my question. "There is a place for the querulous mind, Madame C, especially when a question has been left unanswered."

"Ah, yes. You wanted to know where this notion of 'Don't take it personally' actually comes from? Did I make it up or did your mother author it from somewhere out in the Great Beyond? That's what you're asking?"

"Precisely."

"I don't really know. I just open my mouth and let emerge whatever wants to come out."

"But surely you would agree that it might just be some wise part of you providing that counsel, instead of the ghost of my departed mother."

She nodded. "It is certainly possible that the wisdom of which you speak, Sir Errol, comes from a wise part of me, but if it does I just wish I would occasionally listen to my own advice." She uttered a raucous bark of laughter and was joined in her mirth by Stewart and Freda. Oh, what fun they were having!

I turned to Stewart and said, "Here's what I will do. I will help you clear up the matter with Prince Arthur so that there are no hard feelings at the Palace. In the meantime, I will consider your other proposal carefully. I'll let you know as soon as I possibly can, given the gravity of your request, but at this moment I cannot give you even the tiniest morsel of possibility that I will accept."

Madame C nodded and said, "All right, then, but let me ask you one more question. If you were to be shown a sign that convinced you to overcome your skepticism and give us your assistance, would you be open to such a thing?"

"I suppose so, if it were a sufficiently compelling sign."

"Do you merely *suppose* you would be open to a sign? Or would you *actually be willing* for such a thing to occur?"

Damn her and her infuriating manner! I must have a stern talk with myself at the earliest opportunity, to discover why it appears necessary for me to get caned repeatedly by this tart-tongued little woman. Lady Forsythia and Helga von Munchen had also applied the stick in their own particular way, totaling up three canings now within the past twenty-four hours. I was beginning to wonder if there was some sort of theme developing.

"I'm waiting," she said.

I was too exasperated to do anything but go along. "All right," I said. "I'm willing."

The three of them chuckled.

"I'm glad I can provide so much humor for you, but can you enlighten me as to exactly what you found so funny about what I said?"

Freda gave me a sympathetic squeeze on the knee, which sent a thrill up through my body in spite of the irritation I was feeling. She said, "It was the way you said it, Sir Errol. Like it was the last thing in the world you really wanted to do. It's not so hard, is it, to be open to a sign from the universe?"

"I confess I don't find it quite that easy. I'm not the sort of fellow that goes about looking for signs."

They also found this funny, although again I was somewhat at a loss to perceive exactly why. Suddenly I couldn't wait to get away from all of them, so I stood up and said my goodbyes.

CHAPTER EIGHT

I asked my companion to remain in the cab while I entered Buckingham Palace through the same side door I'd used in my earlier visits. The footman showed me in and turned me over to the butler, who led me into the anteroom of the prince's apartments.

Shortly I was ushered in to the princely presence, finding him sitting at his desk surrounded by the usual clutch of assistants. His main man, Kudlow, shooed the others out and bade me to sit down on a comfortable sofa. In a few moments the prince gave forth a series of harrumphs and came over to join me.

The intention of my visit was to guide him to a higher perspective on his lust and affection for the girl he called Ariana. Before I dropped the guillotine on his tender feelings, though, I wanted to get him, as they say, softened up. It occurred to him that I might do so by discussing a personal matter with him.

"I say, Possum, you've lived an exalted life, though not of course without its share of misery and burden."

He gave me a suspicious stare and said, "I would cautiously agree, although it sounds as if you are leading me somewhere and that always makes me nervous."

"Indeed, Your Royal Highness, I must confess I am. May I have your permission to speak of a personal matter?"

He drew back, obviously surprised. "Well, yes, I suppose so."

"Lately I've been much consumed with questions of mortality."

"You mean the drawing up of wills and such? That is not quite my bailiwick."

"No, not that. I'm talking of deeper questions, such as 'Why am I here?' and 'What potentials do I need to express so that I may feel complete and at ease when death comes calling?"

A look of genuine alarm came over the princely countenance. "Good God, man, you must put a stop to that sort of thing! I believe they call it 'introspection' or something like that. Whatever it is, it's utter rot and will get you nowhere. When the urge for self-reflection comes over me I force myself to go out to the croquet lawn and bash a few balls about until the feeling passes."

"But don't you worry that you are overlooking important aspects of life?"

"Nonsense! I've always avoided any kind of self-awareness and look where it's gotten me." He waved his arms at the sumptuous, royal furnishings around us.

I restrained myself from observing that his great success in life was likely due to other factors. Being born to Queen Victoria might have given him a slight leg up over the competition.

"Quite rightly," I said. "Let's move on to another matter and consider the subject closed. Now, Your Highness, I proceed to my main business. It is with relief tempered by sadness that I come to give you a full report on the remarkable young woman you know as Ariana."

He lurched forward. "Good God! Has something happened to her?"

"She has undergone a profound transformation, Your Highness, but she is in perfect health. In fact, I have brought her to you so that she can talk to you in person."

"That's absolutely splendid, Roller! Where is she?"

"Waiting in a cab outside, but first let me tell you that she has been in retreat at an estate near Blenheim Palace, where she sought solace to do the searching of soul so necessary in great matters of the heart."

"You're confusing me, Sir Errol. Let us bring the girl in and have her tell me herself."

He dispatched Kudlow to fetch Freda; moments later she entered the room with her head ducked demurely, the rest of her body still covered by the cloak and hood she'd worn on the trip in from Blenheim.

The prince cried out, "Ariana!" and leapt to his feet.

"Your Highness," she said, with a bow and curtsy.

"Come and sit down, my dear. Sir Errol, will you help her off with her cloak?"

"With pleasure, Your Highness."

I slipped the bulky cloak off Freda's shoulders, revealing the nun's habit she wore beneath it.

The prince stumbled backwards, sputtering and coughing into his sleeve. "What is this?" he croaked.

I said, "I present to you a changed woman. Your Highness, may I introduce Sister Freda."

To say the prince appeared stunned would be an understatement. His jaw was working but no words were coming out. Finally he sat down with a thud and slumped back in his chair.

"Your Highness," Freda said, kneeling before him and placing both her hands on his knees. The prince snapped upright as if jolted by electricity. "Please let me tell you what has happened," she said.

"All right," he said, his voice hoarse with chocked-back emotion.

Freda wasted no time in spinning the tale we had crafted. She said, "In my time here, Your Highness, I developed special feelings for you. You are a remarkable man."

The prince perked up, looking a bit less morose. Men of a certain age, especially dull and ordinary ones like the prince, love nothing so much as hearing beautiful young women tell them how utterly fascinating they are.

She carried on: "Finally I came to my senses and realized I could not have you as my own. And if I could not have you I would give myself to no other. That's why I fled to the countryside. I needed time to contemplate the true purpose of my life. After much reflection, I found spiritual solace by taking refuge in this nun's habit."

She didn't mention that we bought the nun outfit for sixpence from a hawker on Portobello Road, but it probably wouldn't have mattered. The prince looked so utterly flummoxed that he probably would not have noticed if the Royal Scottish Guardsmen marched through the room with bagpipes blaring.

After stuttering, stammering and emitting a few random harrumphs, the prince gathered himself and said, "We salute the choice you have made to enter the spiritual life. It is not quite the life we might have forecast for you, but we are pleased to be surprised."

"I'm glad you understand, Your Highness," Freda said.

The prince said, "Kudlow, bring a purse." Kudlow fetched it and gave it to the prince, who shook out a handful of gold sovereigns and placed them tenderly into Freda's palm. "Please allow me to make a contribution to your order."

"Why thank you, Your Highness," Freda said, her hand closing around the coins at the speed of a beaver-trap. We said our goodbyes and left, the prince standing in the center of the room scratching the royal head.

Pulling away from Buckingham Palace in the cab, Freda unclutched her hand and revealed six shiny, gold sovereigns. She gave me three, by our prior agreement, which I figured to be fair and reasonable compensation for a morning's worth of private detective work.

Our plan was to stop at my flat for a celebratory cup of Francesca's coffee, then to send Freda on to the train station to return to Blenheim. I was looking forward to a nice nap after she had departed. However, what happened next was radically far from a nap; indeed, it gave me a hard and not entirely welcome shove in a completely different direction.

The moment I unlocked the door of my flat and stepped back into its comfortable environs, I felt an immediate narrowing of my vision. Suddenly everything was closing in on me from all sides and

I could not breathe. It felt like a giant was hugging me so tightly I couldn't expand my chest to get a breath in. Panic washed over me and I felt faint. I managed to stagger over to the sofa and collapse on it. Darkness came over me and the thought flashed through my mind that I was dying. The next thing I knew I was coming back into consciousness feeling my breath coming in and out freely. The giant had released his squeeze and I could breathe again! I sucked air in greedily, feeling delivered from the jaws of death.

Freda was looking down at me with alarm on her face. "Sir Errol! Are you all right?"

I definitely did not feel all right. What was happening to me?

"I don't know," I said. "I've never felt anything like that before."

Freda said, "I believe Dr. Freud would call it an anxiety attack, but I have a different idea."

"Yes?"

"Remember Madame C asking you if you would be willing to receive a sign from the universe?"

"Yes."

"I think you just got your sign."

I started to deny the outrageous possibility of such a thing, but then I thought: what if she's right? I don't mind telling you the idea disturbed my notion of how our dear old world is put together. I began to wonder if I was succumbing to the change in the atmosphere I could feel around me.

There was no question that something was definitely going on. Physics, a subject I had always shunned with the same rigor as I avoided the loathsome vegetable known as okra, had suddenly become the rage of the day. You couldn't go to a party anywhere in fashionable London without hearing people spouting off about time and space, as if they knew what they were talking about.

It brought to mind that odd duck I'd met in Dr. Jung's waiting room on my fruitless trip to Zurich, taken mainly to assure Lady Forsythia that I had a sincere interest in remediating the flaws in my character. After my first disappointing session I was in the waiting room gathering my things to leave when a thirtyish fellow came into the room and plopped down. The chap, whose untamed curly hair was in serious need of a good barber's attentions, said his name was Einstein and that he had arrived early for dinner with Dr. Jung. We struck up a conversation, during which I made the mistake of asking him what line of work he pursued. He went off on a wild ramble about how time didn't work like everybody thought it did and how space was curved like a rainbow and how the stuff he was talking to Jung about was going to change the world.

I tried to set the poor fellow straight, as patiently as I could, that most people didn't give a flying fig about time or space as long as they didn't bump into things or arrive late to the opera. He apparently was bowled over by the power of my argument, because it pretty much shut him up. He just lapsed into muttering in German and started leafing furiously through old magazines.

Now I was beginning to wonder if there was something worth paying attention to in all that prattle. Fortunately I was acquainted with someone who knew everything there was to know about spiritual goings-on around London. Usually I avoided him for just that reason, but it looked like it was time to renew my acquaintance with the maven of all things metaphysical, Bratty Poindexter. His given name was John Paul Poindexter, but a college nickname had been bestowed upon him due to the perpetual expression on his face, which resembled the pout of a spoiled brat.

I called round to his house at a decent hour, half past ten. His butler, whose name I couldn't recall, opened the door and said, "Good day, Sir Errol. It's been a long while since we've had the pleasure of a visit."

"Good day, and please forgive me for forgetting your name, my good man."

"I'm Grimsby, Sir Errol." "Quite right. Grimsby it is, then. I'm here to call on Mr. Poindexter."

Just then I saw Bratty himself, still in his morning robe, coming up the hallway behind his man. He waved to me and called out, "Errol Hyde! Or I should say, SIR Errol Hyde. I don't believe I've seen you since you ascended to the Knighthood."

"Just Errol will be fine, Bratty."

He grinned. 'So it's going to be Bratty and Roller, eh? You must be here to plum the depths of memory in search of some scrap of our now-fading youth. Either that, or you've come to tell me of a sad reversal in your family fortunes and to ask me for a loan to tide you over. If the latter, you would be the third old friend to visit me for that purpose this week."

I forgot to mention that Bratty was extravagantly rich. His old dad, a thrifty Scotsman who relentlessly pinched his every penny until the moment he expired, had owned woolen mills and whiskey distilleries scattered all over the North. Bratty, the old man's sole heir, had wisely cashed in the wool and whiskey businesses in favor of London real estate, of which there is hardly anything realer.

"Nothing like that, Bratty. While I sympathize with the plight of the impoverished aristocrat, I am happily in full flush on the financial front. I'm here on much more pleasant business, and I promise it won't cost you a farthing."

"Well, then, please come in. Grimsby, fetch us a pot of coffee, which I recall to be Sir Errol's preferred libation. Correct, Roller?"

"Indeed, and thank you for remembering, Bratty."

He bade me sit down in the drawing room and took a perch across from me. "Now what is this pleasant business that promises not to lighten the Poindexter purse?"

I told him about my growing interest in the metaphysical and spiritual aspects of life, inspired by the case I was working on. I revealed that Madame C had asked me to be open to a sign from the universe, and even told him of the alarming fainting spell I'd had upon entering my flat.

"I confess to being a late-comer in this area of study, Bratty, and since I know you to be a keen student of metaphysics and spirituality, I would like to ply you with questions and perhaps even ask for an introduction or two."

Bratty seemed genuinely touched. "I'd be delighted. You are the first of the old Cambridge crowd to express any interest in my pursuits. In fact, most of them run away from me at social gatherings when I begin to speak of spiritual matters."

Grimsby came in with our coffee and poured us each a cup. I took a sip and winced inwardly. Why an English butler cannot seem to make a decent cup of coffee is beyond my ability to fathom! However, by adding a double tot of cream and a hefty spoonful of sugar I was able to make it palatable enough to keep my outrage at bay.

"Honestly, Bratty, until recently I might have been counted among their number, but now, though still skeptical, I am beginning to wonder about the very subjects I used to shun."

"Well," Bratty mused, "you are approaching that time in life when men begin to think beyond the physical. One day you look down at your body and realize it won't be here that much longer. You begin to seek a more enduring part of yourself."

I was far from convinced that there actually *was* any sort of enduring part of myself, but I decided it was not the time to argue the point with Bratty. When I was a child various stepmothers had tried to get me to think about my immortal soul but I always arrived back at the same place I started. The way I figured it, either everybody had a soul or nobody did. I reasoned that if I had a soul, even lowly creatures such as fleas had to have one, too.

When I was a lad of nine or ten years old I tried asking stepmother #2, the most religious one of old Dad's wives, about these matters. I said, "I can get to heaven by working on my soul, right?" She agreed wholeheartedly and gave me a big beam of a smile. I was glad to get any kind of smile out of her. Up until then she had only looked at me with a worried, puzzled expression that seemed to say, "What have we here?"

That very day I had seen a hedgehog in the garden and gotten a fleabite when petting a neighbor's dog, so I pressed her further. "Do all of God's creatures have souls or just human beings like us? What about hedgehogs and fleas?"

She assured me that even fleas had tiny souls.

I dove right in to the heart of the matter. "Well, then, if a flea can work his way to a little flea-heaven, does he get there by biting humans, which is his natural tendency, or by refraining from biting them?"

This question must have pushed her past the limits of her theology, because she told me to shut up and drink my tea.

Bratty said, "I'm lunching today with a new lady friend, so perhaps we should get down to your business. How may I help you?"

"It's widely known that you are master and maven of all things metaphysical, Bratty, so I thought that perhaps you might introduce me to some of the 'spiritual crowd.' I want to try out some of these new ways of thinking in hopes of becoming more enlightened in such matters."

"And of course you are hoping also to, as they say, 'crack your case' along the way."

"Just so."

"Very well, then. I believe I actually do detect a hint of sincerity in your request, which is far more than I am accustomed to in my circle of friends. So let's see how we can introduce you to 'spiritual society' so that you can sail about in this uncharted territory with the ease in which you navigate fashionable London society. Perhaps in turn you can show me how to feel less clumsy in that high society world in which you seem to flourish."

"Really? I never thought of you as much interested in the social whirl, Bratty. What of it makes you feel clumsy and awkward?"

"Mainly I detest standing around talking about absolutely trivial matters."

"And what subjects would count as 'trivial matters'?"

"Oh, you know, all that stuff about what plays you've seen and what fabulous new dining establishment you've just been to."

"Ah, yes, I know exactly what you mean."

"I keep waiting for everybody to stop talking about surface trivia and get down to what's really on their mind but it never happens. Am I a hopeless case, Roller?"

"I don't know if I would classify you as 'hopeless,' old friend, but you are certainly lacking in the fundamental requirement for being at ease in high society."

"Which is?"

"The ability to talk with great enthusiasm for long periods of time about absolutely nothing."

"Oh, dear, I see what you mean. Perhaps I am a lost cause."

"Nonsense, Bratty. Anyone can master the art of being utterly vacuous—it's practically a snap! Here's what we'll do. You invite me to one of your spiritual gatherings and I'll take you along to one of the social events I'm obliged to attend. In no time we'll have you prattling on masterfully about nothing at all."

He said, "I would be most grateful . . . I think. As it happens, Roller, I am hosting a dinner party tomorrow night that you would be welcome to attend. Every month or two I invite a group of people to hear a talk from a guest who's got something to say in the metaphysics realm. A sizeable selection of the 'spiritual crowd,' as you call them, will be there, including a few guests from the Continent I have yet to meet. Our guest of honor is a young fellow who seems to be doing some remarkable things with dreams and time."

"Dreams and time, eh? Whatever could that mean?"

"I'm not quite sure, having not met the lad yet, but he comes highly recommended. We'll both have to wait and see. 8 o'clock sharp, then, Roller?"

"I'll be here, and thanks for your assistance, Bratty."

CHAPTER NINE

I felt so good after leaving Bratty's company that I decided to stop by my club for a drink and a round of snooker before heading homeward. Although the weather was turning foul, I thought I might be able to get a good walk in before the heavens opened up. I strutted along at a merry pace all the way over to Shaftsbury Avenue, home of the ancient and venerable Eccentrics Club, arriving just in the nick of time. The first fat drops of a downpour were beginning to splat on my bumbershoot as I legged the last block to the club.

"Good day, Sir Errol," said Phipps, the doorman. He then leaned in and intoned the traditional greeting afforded to all members upon arrival: "True Eccentrics are always welcome here."

"Thank you, Phipps, and a good day to you, sir. Is the old place a-buzz with activity today?"

"Regrettably, Sir Errol, merriment is at a bare minimum. I have opened the door to only three members so far."

"That's just fine by me, Phipps. All I want today is a quiet place to sit and think while I savor a sip or two."

"Then you shall everything you want, Sir Errol, just as it should be." He swung open the door and ushered me in to the tomb-like quiet of my club. Lovejoy, the butler, stepped forth and gave me a welcome bow.

"Welcome, Sir Errol. Where would you like to take your ease today?"

"I think I'll nip into the Library and cajole old Emerson into giving me a taste of some celebratory spirit. I'm having an especially fine day."

"Excellent, Sir Errol. I happen to know that Emerson is all smiles today because he has finally procured another bottle of the Remy Martin from the fabled 1858 vintage."

"My God, that's splendid! Let us proceed with haste." One doesn't usually drink cognac during the daylight hours, but in this case I felt an exception was warranted.

Lovejoy escorted me into the Library bar and got me settled in my favorite overstuffed chair. He arranged an Ottoman at an agreeable angle for me to park my feet on, and then scurried off to give my particulars to the barman. The Library is off-limits to the club's smokers, who must perform their evil and odoriferous habit in the Cigar Bar down the hall. I took a deep breath and settled back into the sumptuous comforts of the chair.

Emerson soon appeared, bearing the snifter of golden liquid on his tray.

"Good day, Emerson. I hear that through your singular and relentless efforts you have procured another bottle of the good stuff."

"Oh, Sir Errol, if I had words to express what a pleasure this is! Not only do I have the joy of pouring a glass of the finest cognac ever made, but I also have the honor and delight of pouring it for our most discerning connoisseur!"

"Thank you, Emerson, although I am far too modest to accept such a designation."

"In any case, milord, may you enjoy it immensely." He drew back to await my first sip.

First I cupped the round-bottomed snifter in my hands and swirled it three times to warm it and release the nose. I inhaled deeply, savoring the essence of the spirit: flowers, honey and a bass-note touch of baked apples. I took my first sip, letting the cognac cascade over my tongue and roll around in my mouth before I swallowed. It was stunning: silky, full-bodied, beguiling. I spontaneously emitted a murmur of deep satisfaction.

Emerson beamed his satisfaction and turned to go back to the bar.

A sudden impulse came over me and I called to him. "Emerson, pour yourself a sip on me."

He looked genuinely alarmed. "Oh, no, Sir Errol. I couldn't possibly . . ."

"Of course you can! It's as simple as pouring some in a glass and tilting the glass so that the liquid slips into your mouth!"

"If only it were that simple, Sir Errol."

"But I'm telling you, my good man, it is just that simple!"

"I cannot imagine what my superiors would say if they knew I had been sampling this precious and costly elixir."

"I shall give you a special dispensation and protect you from any criticism. In any case, your drink goes on my bill, so I can't imagine anyone finding fault."

He shook his head sadly. "No, even if I were to face no disapproval, I don't think I would be able."

"Why on earth not?"

"Honestly, Sir Errol, I'm afraid if I ever tasted anything so grand I would never again enjoy the humble spirits that sustain me on a daily basis. My life would turn into a living hell of disappointment and despair, all because of one sip of cognac."

My goodness! Emerson was a hard case if I'd ever seen one! He was living proof that by mounting a vigorous argument in favor of your limitations, you win the argument every time. With that kind of thinking, our aquatic ancestors would never have climbed out of the water and tried flopping about on dry land. I made a mental note to resist charitable impulses for the rest of the day.

"Very well, then, let me sip my drink in peace, unless you happen to spot Darcy Slatkin skulking about the premises. I missed my billiard match with him the other day and am eager to relieve him of some of the Slatkin fortune."

"I shall keep an eye out for him, Sir Errol, and may the brilliance of your play carry the day."

I sank back in my chair and let another swallow of the golden elixir writhe sensuously across my tongue. If there are any satisfactions in life greater than huddling in the comfortable refuge of one's club, sipping a fifty-year-old cognac on a stormy day, I do not know of them. Despite my affection for the pleasures of hashish, I must award cognac the prize for being most conducive to self-philosophizing. For twenty minutes or so after I quaffed my cognac I basked in the overall rightness of the world. All was good with everything, my place secure in this most wonderful of universes. Rain was pelting the streets outside, the fire was crackling nearby and all was so quiet I could hear the soft clack of billiard balls from far down the hall.

The problem with alcohol is that your golden view of the world fades after twenty minutes, about the time it takes for your liver suddenly to realize you are attempting to poison it. Your liver panics and floods your bloodstream with alarm signals, tiny chemical cease-and-desist orders to stop doing whatever you're doing. You feel a slight irritation forming in your cells along with a hint of disappointment that this wonderful world you inhabited just moments ago could be disappearing in the fog. However, at this very moment a very naughty part of your mind kicks in and suggests a solution to this rapidly encroaching sense of irritation and despair: drink more alcohol!

I thought more highly of my liver than that, so I always left my consumption of spirits to a single snifter of cognac.

I heard a babble of voices in the hall and soon my billiards opponent, Darcy, stuck his nose in the door of the Library.

"Heavens, Roller, is that you crouching back there in the gloom?"

"Indeed, Darcy, I'm mentally preparing for our match. Are you ready to have the massive Slatkin fortune reduced significantly?"

He said, "Step forth, gladiator, and meet your fate."

We spent the next hour jockeying back and forth around the snooker table until I was three pounds, six shillings richer. Afterwards I sunk my winnings into lunch for the both of us, so everything evened out in the long run. Although I have a fondness for billiards, I had another purpose for engaging Darcy's attention. I knew from long standing that while he was addicted to billiards, his overarching passion was for politics, a subject in which I attempt to maintain a condition of blithe ignorance.

While he sawed away at a good cut of beef and drank a bottle of Bordeaux, I pumped him for the latest political gossip. If, according to Madame C, I was destined to change the direction of human history, I figured I ought to at least put in a little time catching up with the old political whirl.

According to Darcy, Europe was rattling along like a rickety old oxcart, just about ready to collapse and dump its occupants in the gutter. That was the good news.

The bad news, as he put it, is that "I can practically smell gunpowder in the air."

I implored him to explain. "And please remember that I am the consummate political boob."

"Where to start? You've got the Ottoman Empire breaking up as we speak, the Young Turks raising hell down in Constantinople while the Bulgarians and other satellite states are suddenly waking up and realizing they're sick and tired of being abused by the Sultan. Then you've got half of Europe in hock to the other half and everybody in hock to the Swiss. Then there's Germany, which is a powder keg waiting to go off if I've ever seen one. When things get like this, there's usually only one solution human beings can reliably be counted on to propose: a war!"

"I see. Going to war takes everybody's attention away from coming up with better solutions."

"Precisely. And, of course, war serves a higher purpose."

"Which is . . ."

"Putting it bluntly, to get rid of excess adolescent males."

"You don't mince words, do you, old friend?" Now that he mentioned it, though, I had actually noticed of late a larger than usual number of lay-about youth lounging around the street corners.

He added, "In nature it's called thinning the herd."

"You're a wise fellow, Darcy, though I must confess your words do not make my heart swell with hope. Now tell me this: how do we Englishmen fit into this current madness you speak of? Is it likely to touch our shores?"

"Are you serious?"

"I told you I'm a bit of a know-nothing when it comes to politics. Please enlighten me."

"Germany would like nothing more than to OWN our shores. Mark my words, Roller: before this thing is over you're going to have us banding together side-by-side with the French to keep the Germans in check."

"Good God, I hope not! I find the French to be off-putting in the extreme, particularly in the areas of attitude and body odor."

"Yes, regrettably the French face is shaped in such a way that a sneer comes naturally to it. As for the vile vapors they emit, these are deliberately brought on by the over-consumption of garlic and shallots."

"Darcy, I marvel at your seemingly endless store of wisdom. Now tell me this: do we have any hope at all on the horizon? While I don't mind an occasional peek at reality, I don't think it's something we should fondle."

He bobbed his head up and down. "Oh, yes, the one hope we can cling to is our new crop of up-and-coming political leaders. Some of these young chaps are quite promising."

"Such as?"

He rattled off some names I recognized such as Lloyd George as well as some I'd never heard before.

"One other question. Now that Lord Asquith has replaced old Campbell-Bannerman as prime minister, do you expect any major changes?"

He made a dismissive little flick of his hand. "Approximately the same change as when you substitute one pair of old shoes for another. One pair may feel a bit more comfortable than the other, but fundamentally you're still dealing with old shoes."

On that less than hopeful note we ended our political discussion. I said, "Now finish that last bite of steak and Let's have a final go at the snooker table."

"With pleasure."

Although I had sworn to avoid charitable impulses, I let him win a pound or two back before I ended up running the table and picking him clean. I left with ten pounds of the Slatkin horde and a head full of political gossip, most of which I tried to forget as soon as I possibly could. The meeting was well worthwhile, however, because while I was listening to Darcy drone on about politics, he mentioned something that, had I not anointed my hair with the carnation-scented pomade I favored, might have caused said hair to stand on end.

In the wake of this revelation I had a particularly brilliant idea flash into my mind, one that exceeded even my own high standards.

CHAPTER TEN

There's an American saying I vaguely recall, something about slaying two birds with one projectile. While crude, in the manner of most things that hale from that raw and savage continent, it does contain a hint of wisdom. Whenever one can combine the useful with the efficient, one gains an advantage that, however miniscule, can sometimes make a difference.

Darcy had electrified my follicles by mentioning an upcoming social event at which all the young political talent would be present and on display. The moment he said it the memory of Madame C flashed through my mind. She had predicted there would be several times to intervene, one of which was a political gathering. The second was a house fire and the third was some sort of romantic event at Blenheim. She said the shaven-headed 'devil' would be present at each event. Of course there could be a dozen political gatherings on the horizon, but it struck me as more than coincidental that Darcy should tell me about one within a short time after Madame C's prediction.

Darcy said he planned to attend, and that I could come as his guest if I wished. He thought it would be an efficient immersion for me into the mysteries of English politics. I had also promised Bratty that I would squire him to a party and help him feel more at ease in the fatuous world of fashionable London. Why not do both at the same time? Bratty was extravagantly wealthy, and it is universally known that politicians love nothing more than a plump, new pigeon to pluck.

I braved the weather in one of the new motorized taxis to call round to Bratty's place again. He came to the door fully dressed and said he was just leaving for an appointment with his tailor. I told him about the political gathering in the offing and asked him if he would attend it with me.

"Next week, you say?"

"Yes, Tuesday evening at Claridge's. Cocktails at 7, black tie."

"Very well."

I told him I would swing by and pick him up.

"Not in one of those, I hope," he said, pointing to one of the new motorized cabs at the curb. "I haven't quite worked up the courage."

"No fears, Bratty. We'll go in a horse-drawn carriage, but I encourage you to try out one of these new beasts. They make an infernal racket, it's true, but they have the advantage of not depositing giant clumps of manure on the streets."

He wrinkled his nose. "I don't like the smell these motorized clatter-traps give off; it's just a different sort of manure, the kind that gets deposited in the air instead of in the gutters."

"You're a sensitive lad, Bratty, and widely admired for it," I said, in hopes of leaving him in a good mood. In actuality, he had been universally ridiculed at Cambridge—a place where ridicule is pretty much the art form and conversational currency of the entire community—due to his difficulties in dealing with even the simplest aspects of ordinary life. Bratty was the only child of older parents who lived in constant fear that something bad was going to happen to their prize offspring; he had grown up in the hothouse atmosphere of a vast mansion staffed with servants who wished nothing more than to fulfill his every need.

When it came time for all upper-class English boys to troop off to boarding school, Bratty's parents kept him at home; they cited the smorgasbord of germs he might encounter as the reason, but it was the unhealthy influences of other boys they feared most. He was privately tutored all the way through secondary school, so when Bratty arrived at Cambridge he hadn't a clue about how the world actually worked. He gained fame from his very first night on campus by a dialogue at bedtime with his roommate that, according to legend, went something like this:

Bratty: "You may extinguish the lamp now."

Roommate: "Do it yourself."

Bratty: "Oh dear—I'm afraid I don't know how."

Bratty was no less sensitive twenty years down the pike from college. Now, though, he also had the full, majestic force of his inherited fortune to apply to his peccadilloes and proclivities.

"Personally," I said, "if I have to choose between stepping in manure and sniffing the occasional whiff of petrol in the air, I'm going to go with the petrol."

"Mark my words, Errol, we'll all pay dearly for this whole oil and gas fad."

"I hear you, Bratty, but if it's all right with you, let's solve that problem another day."

"Very well," he said. "And don't forget tomorrow night. I've added you to the dinner list and given you a prime spot at the table right across from our speaker. Will you be bringing Lady Forsythia?"

"Regrettably, Lady Forsythia and I are somewhat on the outs these days."

"So sorry to hear. However, you enjoy a certain reputation for always having other irons in the proverbial fire. Would you like us to set another place in case you decide to bring another companion?"

"It is unlikely that my fortunes will improve significantly before tomorrow night, but it won't hurt to think positively, now will it?"

"That's the spirit, Errol. We'll set an extra place."

. . .

The next day dawned bright, or so I was told. It was nearly noon when I bumbled my way into the drawing room of my flat for my morning coffee. Francesca took one look at me and said, "You look a bit rumpled, Errol. Did you have a late night?"

"I was troubled by dreams all night long, but now I can't remember any of them."

"Where I come from we call dreams 'thoughts of the heart.' They express the things you don't know how to think about in your mind."

"I hope these weren't coming from my heart. At one point I felt like I was being chased by some large, billowing forms and I couldn't figure out how to escape them."

"See? You're already beginning to remember. Have you thought of keeping a pad by your bed to write them down?"

"No, I hadn't thought of that. Normally I don't care a whit about dreams, but the subject is suddenly looming up everywhere I go."

Francesca said, "I love to think about my dreams. I keep a journal on my bedside table so I can write them down before I forget the details. I've been doing that since I was a teenager. One of my teachers suggested it and I've hardly missed a day since. I have thousands of dreams in my journal."

"How very odd! Just tonight I am dining with a new group of people, among whom the subject of dreams is a great fascination. Indeed, the speaker tonight is some sort of expert on dreams!"

"Oh, Sir Errol, you must remember what he says so you can tell me all about it tomorrow!"

"I have a better idea, my dear. Would you like to accompany me?"

Her eyes opened wide. "Sir Errol! I don't know what to say!"

"Just say yes. That's we need for now."

"Yes! Yes! Yes!" she said, her impossibly long eyelashes all a-flutter with excitement.

I was pleased.

Grandmother Hyde schooled me well that one must always bring a house-gift to one's host, and so it came to pass that at the appointed hour I arrived at Bratty Poindexter's townhouse with a ravishingly gorgeous Italian woman on my arm. I had been waiting all day to see the look on Bratty's face when he saw Francesca for the first time. He was a dedicated connoisseur of feminine pulchritude, as I was, with an especially keen interest in the young, exotic variety. Though he was, as they say, pushing forty, he was still in the overheated throes of adolescence, a case of delayed development due to his hothouse upbringing. So repressed and untutored was he in the area of carnal *amour*, it was rumored that he did not manage to lose his virginity until the ripe age of 28. If true, it would probably qualify as something of a record for a single man of means in London.

Once he dipped his toe in, as it were, he dove in for a full belly flop in the ocean of love. Whenever I saw him out and about he always had on his arm a ravishing Spaniard or an icy-hot Swede or some other exotic bird of paradise. They were always foreign-born beauties in their early twenties, and from a social class at least one notch below Bratty's own. In other words, they were everything Francesca was.

Therein lay the other part of my genius idea: It was high time for Bratty to settle down. In my view, Francesca would make a perfect mate for the old boy. She was lusty, fun and refined all at the same time, a combination that was nearly impossible to come by in the social class to which Bratty belonged. And thanks to my generous tutelage, she spoke a refined brand of the King's English, with just enough of an accent to make her intriguing.

I had supervised her wardrobe choices for the evening with Bratty's tastes in mind. He was a lifelong connoisseur of the female breast, as I was, although our tastes diverged somewhat around magnitude and volume. My special fondness was for the jiggle and sway of voluptuousness, while Bratty's predilections ran more to the pert and nubile, two qualities with which Francesca was spectacularly equipped. She was also wearing the lowest-cut gown permissible in polite society; I had bought it for her at Harrod's, the two of us in consultation with a sympathetic shop-girl as Francesca tried on many different outfits. We finally settled on a fawn-colored silk gown that draped pleasingly over the contours of her form. The cut of the dress allowed Francesca to go without the restricting encumbrance of a brassiere. If you looked hard enough—something I was quite sure Bratty would do—you could even see a pinkish hint of nipple.

We walked into the foyer of Bratty's house and caught sight of our host, who became virtually engorged, body and soul, when he saw Francesca's stunning beauty for the first time. Under normal circumstances one would be tempted to say his eyes popped out, except that one of the distinguishing features of Bratty's countenance was that his eyes always looked popped out. I heard him emit a low, guttural sound similar in tone to the grunts made by the Himalayan mountain goat coming into rut.

"What have we here, Sir Errol?" Bratty asked, his bulging eyeballs devouring every inch of Francesca's form.

"Mr. John Poindexter, it gives me great pleasure to introduce you to Miss Francesca Molinari."

"It gives ME great pleasure, too," he said, his tongue nearly lolling out of his mouth. "Please come in and join us."

There were about fifteen people in the drawing room, which buzzed with conversational chatter and the clinking of wine glasses. I didn't recognize anyone in the room, a situation refreshingly rare in London society, where one tended to see the same old crowd week in and week out. Then I spotted Lady Meredith, who occupied a role in Bratty's life similar to the one Lady Forsythia played in mine. I nodded to her across the room; she favored me with a tiny smile.

The butler took our drink orders: a half-glass of Bordeaux for me, a flute of champagne for Francesca. She and I had already smoked a pipe or two of hashish, in order to get the proper attitude of detached amusement so necessary to maintain when dining among English people. I was afraid that a whole glass of wine would take me out of the zone of detached amusement into a dimension of mirth that might possibly include fits of giggling.

I surrendered Francesca to Bratty, who took her off for a so-called tour of the house, and began my standard figure-8 circuit through the crowd. Right away I could see a difference between this group of psychic enthusiasts and the typical London crowd; the spiritual crowd dressed in a much more imaginative style. Of course, the fundamentals were the same: the men in tuxedos and the ladies in gowns, but it seemed that each person had gone to some length to add a touch of individual flare to their outfit.

One woman wore a shimmering gown that must have cost 500 pounds, accessorized by a red silk scarf casually wrapped around her neck and thrown over one shoulder. She introduced herself as a dancer of some sort, originally from America. Since both dance and America were subjects of little interest to me, I only chatted with her briefly. She seemed quite taken with herself and also was quite drunk already. The only thing I found charming about her was her name, Isadora, one I'd never heard before.

One tall gentleman topped off his traditional tuxedo with a lavender cashmere beret, matched perfectly by a rose of the same color in his lapel button. It was rare to see a man wearing a hat indoors, but somehow his ensemble worked well. For a moment I might have even felt a twinge of envy. Two young men stood beside him, a twitchy-looking twenty-year-old with a little square moustache, and a pale, thin teenager who kept peering around as if wondering, "What am I doing here?"

Halfway through my circuit of the room, however, the mellow mood of my evening got smashed to smithereens.

I introduced myself to a stout gentleman with a beard and pince-nez, who pumped my hand enthusiastically and said how glad he was to meet me.

"I have heard a great deal about your exploits as a detective, Sir Errol," he said, his English tainted by an odd Germanic accent. He gave me a curt bow and said, "My name is Gerhard Gunther, visiting from Bavaria."

I was flabbergasted. "How has a Bavarian gentleman learned of my so-called exploits, Herr Gunther?"

"From my esteemed colleague, Sherlock Holmes. He babbles on endlessly about his admiration for Sir Errol Hyde."

Up until that moment I had been viewing our conversation through a haze of hashish and Bordeaux, but something in his tone snapped me to attention. What was it about this fellow?

Suddenly I felt my face flush involuntarily. "Damn you, Holmes! It's you, isn't it?"

Under the stuffing of his disguise I could see his body shaking with mirth. He gestured for me to step over to the corner of the room and whispered in my ear that he was here on a case.

He said, "Are you here socially or on business?"

"Business," I said. "Could it be the same business as yours?"

"I rather doubt it," he said, "unless you are interested in new trends in German art."

"Not quite my patch of turf," I said, "but what does this evening have to do with German art? I was told that we were to hear a fellow speak about time and dreams."

"Quite correct," he said, "but aren't you going to tell me what you're investigating?"

"I'm sworn to silence," I said, "but I assure you it's a matter of great importance that certainly doesn't touch on German art."

"You might be surprised," he said.

"I doubt it. The only thing that surprises me is how you got invited to this dinner. Is Bratty on to your little ruse?"

"Hardly. I came as a guest of the dancer you were chatting up just a few moments ago. Mr. Poindexter believes me to be Herr Gunther, and I wish to keep it that way. You're not going to let my little secret out, are you?"

"Of course not."

"Excellent, then. We sleuths must stick together. Right, Sir Errol?"

Something in the way he accented the "Sir" in Sir Errol pricked my interest. "Are you still irritated about my knighthood, Holmes?"

"Irritated? I think not. Puzzled? No doubt. Mystified? Most certainly."

Just then Bratty came into the room with Francesca. I noticed her arm was draped casually over his. They made a beeline over to Holmes and myself.

"My dear Sir Errol!" Bratty said. "How fortunate you are to have such a pulchritudinous and delightful a lady friend as your Francesca! She has charmed me utterly."

Francesca batted her impossibly long eyelashes. "Mr. Poindexter was kind enough to show me his magnificent home, Sir Errol, and what a wonderful place it is."

I put on a gallant tone and said, "I'm sure Mr. Poindexter would agree that it is made even more wonderful by your appearance in it." Bratty beamed and bobbed his head up and down. "Please allow me to introduce you to Herr Gunther, a connoisseur of German art."

Holmes bowed to Francesca and said, in his ridiculous accent, that he was pleased to meet her.

Bratty said, "You came with my eccentric friend, Isadora, did you not?"

"Indeed," said the alleged Herr Gunther. "Thank you for allowing me to come as her guest. And now I should be getting back to the lady." He ducked out of the conversation and made off for the other side of the room.

"I should do the same," Bratty said, glancing across the room at Lady Meredith, who was glaring at him with raised eyebrows. No doubt his fascination with Francesca was not going unobserved by his guest of the evening. He turned back to Francesca and said, "Perhaps we could get better acquainted on another occasion when the atmosphere is more serene."

"I would like that," Francesca said, leaning forward to squeeze his hand and give him the best possible angle for viewing the pert peaks of her bosom.

Bratty said, "I'll be in touch, and thank you again for gracing my humble abode with your beauty and charm."

Francesca took my arm and we resumed our socializing, taking care to avoid the side of the room occupied by Bratty's glaring girlfriend. We didn't have to endure much more party chatter before the butler entered and rang a little bell to announce that dinner was served.

The new trend in London dinner parties was to serve the food buffet-style. Once considered outrageously casual by the tuxedo-and-gown crowd, buffet dining was gaining momentum for a variety of reasons, the main one being that it required far fewer wait-staff. I liked it because it didn't waste time and because it gave one an opportunity to get up and move around instead of sitting for two hours.

Francesca and I filed through the line and filled our plates with the evening's fare: Scottish salmon poached in champagne, white asparagus in brown butter, scalloped potatoes and a green salad. I cast my eye about for a dinner roll, but then remembered: Bratty had a peculiar theory about wheat, being firmly convinced it caused all sorts of mental and physical maladies. If you gave him the slightest opening he would go on a rant about something called *gluten*, which he claimed was the true evil that lived in the heart of the poor grain. Accordingly here was a new type of bread on the buffet, one made from rice and barley flour. I picked up a piece and gave the corner of it an experimental nibble. Due to the absence of the dread glutens, it wasn't as chewy as I like my bread to be. In the main, though, it wasn't as bad as one might think.

There was also a huge bowl of trifle standing by for the dessert course; I, for one, couldn't have been happier. It was my very favorite dessert.

Readers, if you are perusing my words in a future time when English trifle has been banned or gone out of fashion, please know there was once a grand dessert comprised of layers of cake, custard, fruit and whipped cream. Often bananas and berries were the fruits employed. The cake would become saturated with the custard, fruit and cream, making for decadent spoonfuls of rich, moist goodness.

Quite frankly, I've always regarded trifle as the taste of heaven on earth. I know full well that my country's culinary insufficiencies are widely lampooned, but I would put the English trifle up against any and all desserts devised by other cultures on our little planet.

But what of the French and their *crème brulee*? Well, I'll tell you what I say: terribly one-dimensional. But wait! What about that bright star in the vast firmament of Italian desserts, the widely admired *tiramisu*? Here I will display a bit of flexibility: *tiramisu* is a step in the right direction, but if you're going to that much trouble why not go all the way? Put some fruit and whipped cream on it, for God's sake!

I took my seat at the table, observing that the place card was inscribed incorrectly with a gratuitous "L" applied to my name, "Sir Erroll Hyde." In my grandmother's time one could have a servant flogged for such an egregious blight upon the social fabric, but nowadays standards have slipped drastically and we must make do with what we have.

Francesca seated herself to my right, with the fellow in the lavender beret to her right. Bratty had positioned himself to my left at the head of the table. Across from me was a place card inscribed, "J.W. Dunne," but his chair was empty. I noted with some chagrin that Holmes was seated to the left of Dunne. Shortly a fellow huffed in, apologizing for being late and looking generally flustered. He sat down across from me and gave a big sigh, as if he had traveled across the desert on a camel to get there. He stuck out his hand and said, "J.W. Dunne." I shook his hand and gave him my name.

"Ah, yes," he said. "Sir Errol Hyde, the eminent detective."

Holmes cleared his throat with a loud *harrumph*, a behavioral tic that Dr. Freud tells us is due to attempting to inhibit a shriek of jealous rage. He reached his bony paw over to shake Dunne's hand, introducing himself in his ridiculous German accent as "Herr Gunther."

Mr. Dunne didn't look to be in the peak of health. Although only in his mid-thirties he had a tremble that one sees more in old men. He was pale and somewhat awkward in his mannerisms, picking at his food listlessly and with the wrong fork. He must have noticed my scrutiny because he said, "My appetite isn't the best tonight. I'm recuperating from some digestive difficulties."

I murmured my sympathies and changed the subject. "I understand you will elucidate the mysteries of time and dreams for us tonight. I'm curious about how you came by your expertise in those particular subjects. Are you a philosopher by vocation?"

"Heavens, no," he said, coming out of his slouch and sitting upright. "I am an aeronautical engineer."

Holmes, or I should say "Herr Gunther," broke into the conversation. "I perceive that you have been in South Africa not too long ago, and hazard a guess that your digestive difficulties might be the lingering result of typhoid fever you contracted there."

Dunne's eyes went wide. "My goodness! How could you possibly know that?"

"And you were no doubt a combatant in the Boer War when you came down with your affliction," Holmes said, a smug look of utter satisfaction on his face.

It was typical Holmes parlor-trickery, designed to mystify onlookers and get them to believe he was in possession of superhuman capabilities. I fired back, "You are probably drawing inferences from the watch-fob Mr. Dunne wears, made of a variety of warthog leather found only in the southern-most portion of the African continent."

Holmes glared at me over the top of his pince-nez glasses, letting me know I had landed a punch.

Dunne glanced down at his watch-fob and said, "You're absolutely right. I had it made when I was recuperating from my bout with typhoid." He turned back to "Herr Gunther" and asked, "How did you know I suffered from that awful disease?"

"Elemental logic, my dear sir. It is widely known that many English troops came down with typhoid in that misguided military adventure. Equally well known is that the typhoid sufferer often continues to feel the effects of the disease long after the main symptoms have been cured."

I was already fed up with Holmes' silly games, but he wasn't through yet by a long shot.

He peered through his fake glasses at Dunne and said, "How are the plans for your gliding aircraft coming along?"

Dunne sputtered. "Goodness! Where did you learn about that?"

In a refreshingly rare exhibit of honesty Holmes said, "I read about it in a newspaper."

"Really?" Dunne said, clearly surprised.

"Yes, a military newspaper to which I pay close attention."

"Ah, then, someday you must tell me how an art enthusiast comes to read 'The Military Times,' but for now tell me what you think of the general idea."

"Ingenious," said Holmes, "although I lack the technical skills to evaluate your designs with the informed thoroughness they deserve."

What was this? Under ordinary circumstances, humility was not to be found within a hundred yard radius of Sherlock Holmes. Yet, here he was, publicly admitting not to know something! I could scarcely believe what I was hearing.

Dunne lit up like the proverbial Christmas tree, his unsettled stomach obviously in remission. I had a feeling he was going to launch into a longwinded explanation of flying machinery, which I and other sentient people knew to be a temporary fad at best, but before he could continue with this tedious line of conversation, I took over the wheel and steered it back on a suitable course.

"Please tell us, how did an aeronautical engineer take an interest in dreams?"

Holmes gave a snort, but Dunne turned back to me and said, "Oh, yes, we must remember our main subject of the evening. The answer, as I will elucidate in more detail when I speak tonight, is that I had a dream, in the wee hours of a Tuesday, of an odd event. That event happened in real life the next day."

"What was this 'odd event' you dreamed of?"

"It was a nightmare, something I might only experience once a year in ordinary life. In my dream I was walking down a path between two high walls when I saw in a neighboring field a horse that had apparently gone mad. It was frothing at the mouth, bucking and plunging about in a most frenzied manner. The horse broke out of the fence and began to chase me down the path. I fled like a hare, and as the horse was about to overtake me I awoke from the dream."

"Remarkable," I said. "And you say this same event actually happened to you the next day?"

His head bobbed up and down. "I was on a fishing trip with my brother when this dream occurred. Over breakfast I regaled him with the details of the dream, which he found as unusual and striking as I did. Later in the morning, as we were walking down a path to the river in which we intended to fish, my brother pointed to a nearby field and said, 'There's your horse.' I chuckled, thinking he was joking, but then saw that he was not. The horse was bucking and running about, giving great snorts of foam out of its mouth."

"Most remarkable," I said.

"That wasn't all. The horse came lunging in our direction, frightening both my brother and myself, but eventually it turned in another direction and ran off."

Holmes sniffed and said, "Very likely a coincidence."

Francesca leapt into the conversation. "No! It's not a coincidence. I've had many dreams that foretold the future!"

"You have?" Dunne said, leaning forward with excitement written all over his face.

"Yes. I've kept a dream journal since I was a girl. Probably at least once a week I dream of something that happens later in real life. I thought it was something everybody did."

"By Jove!" Dunne said. "That's exactly what I think. Would you be willing to share some of your findings with me? I'm writing a book on the subject."

"Certainly," Francesca said. "They're just dreams."

Dunne said, "They're much more than dreams, my dear lady. If we dream of things that have not happened yet, it rearranges all the known laws of physics!"

Holmes wasn't having any of it. "Nonsense," he said. "Thanks to the investigations of one of our most esteemed countrymen, Sir Isaac Newton, the universe is laid out in a most orderly fashion. Tick-tock-tick-tock—that's all we need to know about time."

Dunne grew visibly agitated. "I cannot agree. I feel that we are the beginning of a whole new understanding of the universe. Have you not heard of the mathematical explorations of Albert Einstein?"

"Mere drivel," Holmes said, exciting a wave of twitches in Mr. Dunne.

"Is this Einstein perhaps a Swiss fellow?" I asked.

"Quite right," Dunne said.

"Then I've met him. He was coming to have dinner with Dr. Jung."

Dunne virtually leapt to attention. "You've met Jung, too?" Dunne asked, looking extremely impressed.

"Yes, of course."

"Goodness, how I wish I could have been part of that conversation," Dunne said.

"Don't fret about it," I said. "I don't think there's anything to learn there, and besides, both of them are rather full of themselves."

I noted that Dunne's eyes were blinking rapidly, no doubt attempting to digest the richness of my repartee'.

He said, "What do you mean by 'full of themselves'? I'm not quite familiar with the phrase."

With no intention to gossip, but merely to enlighten, I shared a tidbit I had gained from my brief sojourn to Jung's home. "Jung has an odd notion of what constitutes a family dinner. He requires both his wife and his mistress to dine together along with him and the rest of the family."

Dunne broke into a fit of coughing, his face turning pink in the process. Even Holmes seemed taken aback. He immediately turned to his left and transferred his attention to the fellow with the beret, leaving Dunne to Francesca and myself. Dunne recovered and bent his head to talk to Francesca about her dream journal.

I noticed out of the corner of my eye that Bratty was observing the communion between Dunne and Francesca with less than beaming approval. His already-thin lips were pursed so tightly they resembled more a horizontal line drawn by a pencil. I glanced down to the other end of the table, where he had stashed his own companion of the evening, Lady Meredith, and saw that she was glaring at Bratty as intently as he was glaring at Dunne. It was time for an intervention.

I stood up and clinked my spoon on a wineglass to get everyone's attention. "Ladies and gentleman. I would like to propose a toast to our host for the evening, Mr. John Poindexter! Let's drink to our good friend in gratitude for his hospitality and the wonderful, varied nature of his friends!" I was rewarded with polite applause and a "Hear, Hear" or two. Everyone raised a glass and drank to our host, except for the fellow in the beret and his two young companions, neither of whom appeared to partake in alcoholic beverages. The three of them simply acknowledged our host with a kind of stiff-armed salute.

Bratty snapped out of his trance of disapproval, put down his wineglass and stood up somewhat unsteadily to receive his accolade. "Thank you, Sir Errol, and thanks to all of you for gracing my humble abode tonight." There were a few chuckles at his "humble abode" comment. The only thing humble about Bratty's opulent abode might be the somewhat skimpy number of proper hand-towels in the guest bathrooms. In my view, the guest bathroom is a place where one should overdo it a bit.

Bratty went around the table introducing the guests. By then I had met all of them except the tall fellow in the beret and his two young companions. Bratty introduced him as Dietrich Eckart and invited him to introduce the two young men. Eckart introduced the overheated little fellow with the square moustache as an artist from Austria and the thin, pale one as a chess prodigy. Dietrich Eckart had a high nasal voice and a pronounced lisp, making it almost impossible to understand their names, which were, in any case, German and utterly unpronounceable.

Eckart said that, having no children of his own, one of his pleasures was squiring promising young people around Europe. The young chess prodigy, Franz something, was about 15 years old and looked like he was trembling all over inside his ill-fitting suit. I had the fleeting thought that he was not often exposed to the light. The artist, Adolf something-or-another, was just past his teenage years and was the opposite of the chess player in temperament. He bristled with angry energy, much like a caged weasel, and looked like he could barely stay in his seat. When introduced he gave a curt nod and returned his attention to his plate.

Bratty finished his introductions and sat back down heavily. He called for a refill of his wineglass and guzzled half of it in one swallow. Francesca and Dunne fell back immediately into their animated conversation about dreams. Glancing to my left I noted the pout on Bratty's face growing more extreme. I felt we might be headed for some sort of *contretemps*. Bratty was widely known for his inability to control his temper. On more than one public occasion he had plumped down on the floor like a toddler and bawled out his rage, once spectacularly at Sotheby's when he was out-bid on an Empire chair. Indeed, his temper was the very reason he had never been admitted to The Eccentrics Club, even though he had petitioned for membership many times over the years. He was always voted down, because nobody wanted to face the inevitable prospect of having to lug a fourteen-stone, 40-year-old braying baby off the premises.

I could feel a slight tug-of-war going on inside myself. Part of me wanted to calm Bratty down and get on with the evening's proceedings. Another part of me, however, had a fiendish little desire to see what kind of amusing mayhem could be stoked up. After all, don't we all have a sacred duty to turn our otherwise ho-hum lives into a bit of theater now and then?

I leaned over and whispered to Bratty, "I see how attracted you are to Francesca. Are you going to just sit there and let Dunne circle her like a shark?"

It was like someone—in this particular case, me—had dropped a hot iron ball down Bratty's throat. His jaw started working like a steam engine laboring up a hill.

"By God, no!" he hissed back at me, "but should I mount a vigorous attack on him, or simply ignore him and woo her with a charm offensive?"

"In the spirit of a harmonious dinner party I would suggest the latter, although this tender approach may not meet your own high standards for a chivalrous rescue."

In truth, Bratty was the last person one might ever suspect of an act of chivalry, his pudgy body more suited to an afternoon of bridge than a bout of jousting. You would never have known it from his house, though—the walls were decorated with coats of arms, old broadswords, chain mail armor and other trappings from the era of chivalry. He was known to be a keen student of Arthurian legend, so I had a feeling that an appeal to his chivalrous nature might produce a result that at least had amusement value.

Bratty chose the chivalrous route. He had sunk a good quart of Bordeaux by then, so when the Great Knight lumbered to his feet to do battle with the forces of evil that threatened his castle, he managed to get to his full height only with a series of wobbles and lurches. By the time he had mounted his imaginary steed and was battle-ready, the table had fallen silent and all eyes were on him.

He thundered, "A man must protect the sanctity of his castle! Mr. Dunne, how dare you enter these premises and attempt the rape of one of my guests!"

Lady Meredith let out a piercing shriek from the other end of the table. Dunne, the accused rapist, sputtered madly, shaking his head from side to side saying "No, No, No!" He gripped the arms of his chair for support, as if an earthquake were swaying the room. On the positive side of things, a sudden surge of color had chased the sickly pallor off his face.

Lady Meredith got up abruptly and stamped her foot. "Good God, Bratty, stop this right now! Sit down!"

"No!" he bellowed. "Not tonight, Meredith! This night I will not allow you to stunt the full stature of my manliness!"

Lady Meredith uttered a garbled screech and strode toward the door. "You'll pay dearly for this," she said. By the time she reached the door she had recovered her usual arch expression. She stopped and fixed him in a fierce glare. "You are doomed, Bratty Poindexter! I shall personally see to it that you are not invited to next year's Cotillion!" She stormed out, her terrible threat lingering in the air like a humid cloud of beer-fart.

Bratty roared, "STUFF YOUR COTILLION!" He turned back to his guests, made a hand-washing gesture and said, "Good riddance." He smacked his lips with satisfaction and called to the butler, "Rigby, we'll have our trifle now!"

Most of the guests were sitting in stunned silence, some even with mouths hanging agape. Holmes was shaking with mirth under his burly padding and Herr Eckart was staring down at his plate with a bitter little smile on his face. The dancer, Isadora, seemed to be enjoying the whole thing immensely, even though, having downed by my observation at least two bottles of Bordeaux, she had adopted a lopsided grin and was sliding down a bit in her chair.

Holmes turned to Eckart and began speaking to him in German, a language I was forced to study for two long years during my schooling. I caught a few words of their conversation but they were talking about German politics, a subject of no interest to any sensible English person.

It was Mr. Dunne I was most concerned with. After Bratty's unhinged caning of him, Dunne had withdrawn into himself and now sat frozen, watching Rigby ladle out trifle. Dunne was clutching his dessertspoon so tightly I could see his knuckles turning white. I caught a sideways glance from Francesca, who leaned over to whisper in my ear: "Is this the way upper class people always behave?"

"Perhaps a bit more rowdy than usual, my dear, but still well within norms. Would you like to leave? I think our chances are slender of hearing a cogent lecture from Mr. Dunne tonight. Let's duck out after dessert."

I wasn't about to leave without my trifle, and I am pleased to report that it did not disappoint. In addition to savoring many spoonfuls of its rich and gooey goodness, I had the great pleasure of introducing Francesca for the first time to its delights. She made the appropriate pleasure-sounds and pronounced it to be "like tiramisu, only better!"

After dessert Francesca had a whispered conversation with Bratty, bent toward him so as to give him maximum opportunity to ogle her pert nipples. It didn't take long to get him back in a jovial mood. I gave my address to Mr. Dunne so he could contact Francesca about her dream journal. Dunne was still stunned by Bratty's onslaught and couldn't say much except to stammer out a "thank you." Shortly he stood up, muttered an apology to the table and fled.

On the way home Francesca pressed me further. "Aren't the upper classes supposed to set an example for the peasants, so as to give us common folk something to aspire to?"

"Yes, I believe that is one of the main pillars on which the class system rests."

"It's not working very well, is it?"

"I fear not. However, dear Francesca, I hope this event doesn't dampen your enthusiasm for the upward ascent for which you are so justly qualified. Being rich isn't completely bad—in fact, it has many salubrious features. At its best it enables a certain indolence conducive to creativity."

She assured me the evening hadn't diminished her zest in any way, and later, after we arrived back home, she was also able to perceive that I was a bit too wrought up from the party to have an easeful transition into sleep.

She inquired, "Sir Errol, could I offer you a hand in helping you relax from the rigors of the evening? It might encourage deep sleep and delightful dreams."

"I like the way you think, Francesca. Your concern for my wellbeing touches me deeply."

"It's the least I can do to express my gratitude for your unique style of mentoring, Sir Errol."

Working together we were able to bring the evening to a climax in a timely manner, and as I was drifting off to sleep I heard her singing softly in Italian as she left to go down to her flat.

CHAPTER ELEVEN

I woke up the next morning feeling chipper and bright. A dream was just slithering away as I opened my eyes, something about a house catching fire and a fellow rushing back in to the flames to get a piece of precious art. I jotted it down so I could tell Francesca about it when she came up with my coffee.

Casting an eye outside and seeing something that resembled sunshine, I decided it would be an ideal day to cavort about a bit in nature. As soon as I had that delightful idea, however, a guilty thought nipped my good feeling in the bud: you need to have a talk with Lady Forsythia. Certain things had been brewing inside me that needed a good airing-out. As I was getting into my robe and slippers I realized a heavy mood was settling over me. How could I have felt so tip-top one moment then deflated myself with a single thought? It made me wonder if I had some sort of upper limit on feeling good, such that I administered the slap of a critical thought whenever I caught myself feeling too good.

I ventured out to give the air a sniff and get my copy of the *Times* off the porch. An overnight downpour had cleansed the streets; the lingering moisture in the air carried a sweet, fresh scent. I gulped a few lungs of oxygen to see if I could chase the fog that had penetrated me when I contemplated talking to Forsythia. The air helped, but I realized I probably wouldn't restore the good feeling in myself until I had my talk with her.

I stooped to pick up my copy of the *Times* and saw the solution to my problem right there in the lower left hand corner of page one. A small headline read: *Kew Gardens Succulent Exhibit Opens Today.*

Succulents! The plants that were once considered too salacious for public viewing were now getting their due day in the royal gardens! I happened to know that few things excited Lady Forsythia more than the observation of succulents. I thought perhaps if I had my conversation with her while ogling the Kew's display of succulents she would be in a better mood to appreciate my utterances.

Anything involving gardens fascinated Lady Forsythia, but it was succulents that unleashed the full torrent of her passion. My cursory reading of Dr. Freud's hypotheses gave me an appreciation of why she might be drawn to the juicy, plump form of the typical succulent. Oddly enough, when I broached these penetrating insights to her she never encouraged me to elaborate on them.

Francesca popped in with my coffee while I was still in my bath, just in time to give my back a thorough and vigorous scrubbing. She told me that Bratty had already sent a courier that morning, inviting her to stop in for tea later in the day. I gave her a few helpful suggestions about how to deal with the most insufferable aspects of Bratty, and then sent her off with a hint or two about the employment of her awesome charms on Bratty. I believe the phrase I used was, "Make him ache for it."

Francesca assured me that she had the keenest intention to dole out her charms in a way that guaranteed Bratty's interest would remain at full attention for the foreseeable future. However, she did express a concern and potential problem. "Don't gentleman expect the object of their affection to be a virgin, Sir Errol?"

I looked her straight in the eye and gave her a bit of enlightenment on the subject: "Dear Francesca, as your mentor I must impart an important bit of wisdom to you: you're always as much of a virgin as you make up your mind to be!"

"Why, Sir Errol! What an unusual point of view!"

"But nevertheless a handy one, my dear. My suggestion is not to let him near your deepest wellspring of charm until he has spent a generous chunk of the Poindexter fortune on a diamond ring and slipped it onto your finger. Until then make do with substitutes, but do not allow him to slide into the ultimate comforts of the true home he will so desperately seek. You are something of a Michelangelo in the manual arts, Francesca, so by all means give him a stroke or two now and then to keep his affections from wandering."

"Sir Errol, your counsel as always is wise and gratefully appreciated. Is there anything I can do to express my appreciation?"

"Your delicious coffee and excellent back-scrubbing have set me up just fine, my dear. I'm shortly off to Kew Gardens, so if I don't see you again before tea, I hope you have a fine time with Bratty."

"Will do, Sir Errol."

After she left I soaked for a while longer, congratulating myself on my successful launch of Francesca into the upper reaches of the London caste system. Mentoring becomes me, I found myself musing as I toweled myself off. Perhaps after Francesca flies the coop I will take on the responsibilities of another charge.

. . .

I occupied myself with those and other pleasant thoughts all the way over to Lady Forsythia's house, but my serene mood was dampened slightly when Forsythia's housekeeper, Myrtle, stuck her nose out the front door and informed me, in her raucous Cockney accent, that the lady of the house was indisposed.

"Is she ill?" I asked.

Myrtle cackled and said, "I don't think you could rightly call it that."

I slipped a shilling into her hand. "Is her indisposition due to her current bout of irritation and disaffection for me?"

"I wouldn't know nuffin' about that, Sir Errol."

I heard footsteps stomping up the hall behind Myrtle. Forsythia pushed open the door all the way and shooed the housekeeper aside.

"What are you doing here at this odd hour, Errol?"

I could see that she was trembling slightly and breathing rapidly, as if I'd interrupted her partway through a program of exercise. However, I'd never seen Forsythia engage in any form of exercise except for her polite and restrained sidestroke in the natatorium.

"I took the liberty of dropping in unannounced because I was seized with an idea! I've come to ask you to accompany me to Kew Gardens. According to the front page of The Times, the royal gardens will this very day unveil the new display of succulents."

Instead of the thrill of joy I expected to see coursing through her, I saw what looked like a headshake of exasperation. Behind Forsythia I heard a wispy, ethereal voice say, "What is it, Sissy dear?"

Sissy? Who would dare address Lady Forsythia Highgate with such a nickname as "Sissy?"

Suddenly a long, lugubrious face peeked over Forsythia's shoulder. It took me a moment to realize who it was. I said, "Oh, hullo, Virginia." She was a writer of some sort whom I'd met at parties here and there around London. I had always avoided her; she was a dreadful boor, always going on earnestly about literature, poetry, women's rights and that sort of thing. I made a mental note to consult a dermatologist someday to find out why earnest people cause such an irritating sensation under my skin.

She said, "It's *Sir* Errol now, isn't it?"

"Yes, but never mind all that. What are you doing here?"

Forsythia stepped back from the doorway and emitted one of her trademark heavy sighs. "I suppose you should come in," she said.

When I stepped into the foyer I saw that both of them were wearing dressing gowns, even though it was closing in on noon. What was going on here? Had I interrupted some sort of slumber party?

They proceeded to inform me otherwise.

"Virginia and I are in love," Forsythia announced, glaring defiantly at me as she clutched Virginia's hand. Virginia just looked on, her sad doe eyes conveying her usual mournful expression.

I was stunned, of course, but as the full import of her news sank in, my heart made a joyful leap. By Jove, this was an excellent turn of events! It rendered needless a conversation with Forsythia I'd been dreading—at Kew Gardens I had planned to broach the subject of ending our engagement. It also spared me the agony of an afternoon staring at succulents. Pretending to be interested in plant life is one of the most stressful pretenses of all.

"Well, Errol—don't you have anything to say?"

"Yes, of course, Forsythia, or should I call you, 'Sissy'? I was quite naturally stricken to inner silence by the ramifications of your utterance."

"Bugger your utterance," Virginia said. "Sissy, why do you care what he thinks about our love?"

"Please, my dear Virginia! Errol is, after all, my betrothed. I have affection for him."

Virginia made a pouty face and said, "I don't see how."

They were discussing me like I was a potted plant they'd recently purchased.

"Don't be so bossy," Forsythia said.

Virginia shot back, "Me bossy? Hah! You're the bossy one, Sissy!"

I had a feeling this could go on for a while. I cleared my throat to remind them that I was standing there, too. "Let me simply offer you both my sincerest congratulations. I salute your new love, but now I must withdraw so that I may console myself in private. It's not every day that a man has his matrimonial dreams summarily dashed."

They gave me a curt nod of dismissal without missing a beat of their bickering. With great relief I set sail and hastened away from their little Isle of Lesbos. The day was a fine one, with only high wisps of clouds against the blue sky, so I chose to hike all the way back to my flat. After the surprise of my visit to Lady Forsythia wore off, I noted that my step seemed a little lighter than usual. In fact, I was bounding along Sloane Street like a border collie off the leash.

I was relieved that I didn't have to put myself through the grinder of Forsythia's anger and disappointment. But I also felt a genuine sense of wishing her well with her new adventure. Even though she had lied to me and concealed her passions for Virginia apparently for some time, I didn't feel a trace of rancor. I'm all for love in whatever forms it shows up in, although I found myself worrying a little about how they were going to introduce their own particular brand of love to the gossiping class to which we all belonged. Intimacies between women were sometimes hinted at, but they were largely thought to take place among lady poets in the far reaches of the Lake District.

Dear Reader, I must confess that, far from disapproving of Lady Forsythia and her affections for Virginia, I found the whole scene somewhat titillating. It gave me a bit of merriment picturing the two of them in bed engaging in the old wiggle-and-tussle. It also provided a tickle of amusement to think of how they would manage their social obligations. Forsythia occasionally supped with the King and Queen; I gave myself quite a giggle picturing Forsythia strolling into the royal dining room with the perpetually mournful Virginia drooping over her arm.

After calling round to my flat to freshen up, I took another brisk walk over to the Eccentrics Club, where I applied myself to a vigorous afternoon of snooker. I also announced my new bachelorhood to my compatriots at the club, thus guaranteeing that the news would be spread all around London by nightfall. I expected a virtual tidal wave of interest from persons of the female persuasion now that I was back on the market.

Then as dusk fell on my Saturday evening, I hauled my body—fatigued by the events of the day and a particularly strenuous final round of snooker—back to my flat to tuck in early. I was in my pajamas with a good book by 8 p.m. and snoozing like a baby by 9.

CHAPTER TWELVE

The next morning I awoke to the sound of a strong wind rattling the windows. I peeked outside and saw the trees whipping back and forth. The morning sky looked dark gray and leaden with impending rain. As soon as I opened the curtains the first fat drops were splattering against the windows.

By the time I had bathed, dressed and enjoyed a cup of Francesca's delicious coffee, a genuine downpour was underway. I had planned to go out on detective business, to make some observations among the crowds entering and leaving morning services at Westminster Cathedral. My visit would also serve a dual purpose, the social benefits of being seen amongst the worshippers without actually having to attend the service.

Fortunately Francesca not only brought me a carafe of coffee—she also came bearing an amusing anecdote about her tea with Bratty.

In true Bratty fashion he had squired her on a tour of the artwork in the house, with particular attention to a Leonardo portrait that graced the master bedroom. As she was lost in rapture over the Leonardo, Bratty toppled her over onto the bed and placed his fleshly body atop her.

"That he climbed on top of me didn't surprise me, Sir Errol, because you had schooled me wisely in Mr. Poindexter's unsubtle approach to romantic union. What happened next did, however, catch me a bit off guard."

"Oh, dear! Tell me more."

"Well, it was probably because he was wearing velvet trousers."

"Beg pardon?"

"I told him in a nice way that I could not be wooed in that fashion. He relented, but before he got up he proceeded to rub his lower body on my thigh. After two or three strokes against the soft velvet the erect and potent form of his manliness lost its composure, making like Mount Vesuvius in his pants. He rolled over on the bed with a groan and fell fast asleep."

"My goodness, that sounds extreme even for Bratty. However, Francesca dear, you must take it as the highest of compliments. He's obviously besotted with you, but beyond that, you asserted your virtue while at the same time giving him a measure of satisfaction! That's an absolutely capital result! How long was he out?"

"He awoke a few minutes later, very apologetic, and asked me if I'd like to resume my tour of his art collection. I begged off politely and let him know I'd be delighted to see more on another occasion."

"That's just fantastic! He'll feel guilty and indebted to you for sparing him embarrassment. You've set the hook most marvelously, my dear! But before we go further, tell me this: given what you know about Mr. Poindexter so far, can you see yourself as wife and lady of his manor or does the thought revolt you? In other words, shall I call off my matchmaking efforts vis-à-vis Bratty and direct my attentions to finding you another suitable gentleman?"

"Oh, no, Mr. Poindexter is entirely suitable. I even find him amusing. He just needs a bit of discipline."

"I couldn't agree more, and I think much of London society would concur! However, I've only seen the gentle side of you. Do you consider yourself enough of a specialist in the disciplinary arts to take on such a project as Bratty?"

"I believe so. In my teenage years an older gentleman took an interest in me and provided funds for my education at a private high school. All he required in return each week was for me to apply a few red streaks to his buttocks with a buggy-whip while he pleasured himself."

"I'm sure you agree that it was a minimal requirement in exchange for the great benefits of a private education."

"Of course—more than generous for the effort required, and much more rewarding than giving neighborhood boys a tug-job for a hundred *lira* a pop."

Sometimes Francesca gave a bit more detail than absolutely necessary, but I was certain that another year or two in London society would cure her of the tendency to make spontaneous utterances in general and about her sexual history in particular.

"Is the gentleman who required your disciplinary attentions still alive?"

"Sadly, no. His noble heart gave out one day in the heat of competition on the bocce ball court. Why do you ask?"

"I was going to suggest writing him a thank-you note. So many of today's youth graduate from secondary school without a single marketable skill. At least you learned something that would come in handy later in life."

"Sir Errol, you've done it again! I have always felt somewhat ashamed of that interlude in my life. You've made me feel happy and proud about something I used to feel guilty about!"

"Well done, my dear. I've found it an absolutely essential life skill, the ability to feel wonderful all the time even though we've done appalling things in the past."

The rain had not relented by the time Francesca went back downstairs. Given the raging elements outside, a wiser man would have simply smoked a bowl of hashish and devoted himself to lofty pursuits. However, I had imbibed nearly a full carafe of Francesca's potent coffee, and as a result felt like a racehorse snorting and bucking in the starting gate. My next official engagement was not for two days, when I planned to squire Bratty to the political gathering. Now that Francesca had entered the picture, though, I wasn't at all sure he would still be interested.

Grandmother Hyde used to say, "When in doubt, just *do* something, and if you can't think of anything to do, make a list."

Grandmother was a great proponent of the healing value of making lists, a custom I did not often practice. Indeed, on occasion I had mounted an argument with the sainted lady, to the effect that making a list put something of a crimp in the creative possibilities of the moment. Her argument in return was that my creative possibilities often cried out for a bit of crimping.

She and I had many differences in our opinions, most of them involving my character. "You spend far too much time just bumbling around, Errol. You must learn to be more purposeful in your activities. And it all starts with the list."

"But Grandmother, bumbling about *is* doing something. If one bumbles around enough something is bound to happen!"

She would just shake her head and mumble something about hoping I didn't turn out like my father. That always stopped any argument between us, because if there was anyone who didn't want me to turn out like my father more than my grandmother, it was I. In fact, my mind was occupied constantly in making sure I didn't turn out like my father, a man who had gone far beyond bumbling into a dimension of aimlessness that few rich slackers ever achieve.

Pondering the rain outside, and no doubt inspired by my grandmother's wisdom.

I was seized by a bold idea: Instead of huddling indoors on this stormy day, I would bundle up, rain slicker and all, and set myself against the elements for a good, long walk. On that walk, as I pitted myself against the relentless adversity of the storm, I would apply the other part of Grandmother's wisdom. I would make a list.

With the rain thrumming on my sturdy umbrella, snug inside my slicker and striding along briskly in a pair of well-made boots, I was feeling, if not on top of the world, at least within yodeling distance of it. Within a few blocks my head had cleared marvelously and a host of questions were leaping gazelle-like through my mind.

Exactly what was the central problem, anyway? Was it that something terrible was going happen, foretold by dreams and visions of Madame C, unless I intervened in some unspecified way? Or was the real problem my own gullibility—had I fallen for some scheme cooked up by Madame C's overheated imagination?

I could feel that my resolve to investigate the matter had slipped by a notch or two. Perhaps another trip out to Blenheim was in order, to shore up my faith and see if I could glean any more useful bits of information. Also, to be frank, the charms of walking in a pouring rain were beginning to wear off a bit. Suddenly a cozy train ride seemed like a very good idea, so I directed my footsteps toward the train station, pausing at a café along the way to consume a hearty three-egg omelet, with bacon and buttered crumpet on the side. Then I climbed aboard the train and rattled off to Blenheim.

By the time I got there the rain had slacked off to a misty drizzle, but the citizens of Blenheim had not yet emerged from their burrows. The streets were deserted save for a lone cabbie in front of the station.

"Ride for the gentleman?" the cabbie called.

I reluctantly climbed aboard. Taxis powered by petrol hadn't made it to the environs of Blenheim, so I was forced to endure a half hour aboard a clattering, yawing carriage drawn by an ancient hay-burner. As we rattled up to the door of Malcolm Stewart's cottage a guilty thought flittered through my mind: I still had not made the list I'd set out to construct. Once again I had engaged in that practice so loathed by my saintly grandmother, of just bumbling around.

As a social call, this particular episode of bumbling around turned out to be an utter dud. I gave a knock at the front door; when no answer came, I took a walk around the premises. The place was deserted.

I sat down on the low stone fence that surrounded the property so I could have a proper think. Where had Malcolm Stewart decamped with his merry band of tricksters? Or perhaps I was giving them too much credit. Maybe it was Malcolm and his band of hucksters.

The cabbie blew his whistle and shouted, "Do ye want me to stay, mister?"

I signaled a 'Yes' to him and continued my pondering. A noise behind me caught my attention and I turned to see a young girl trooping through the woods in my direction, accompanied by a floppy-eared hound trudging along by her side. She looked to be about twelve or thirteen years old and was dressed in simple clothing. She gave me a friendly wave.

"Hallo," she piped. "Are you Sir Errol?"

To call me surprised would be to understate the case.

"Indeed I am. And who might you be, young lady?"

She came over and hiked herself up to perch on the wall beside me. "I'm Freddy, sir. It's Fredericka really but everybody calls me Freddy." She pointed to her dog and said, "This is Humphrey. He goes with me everywhere."

"Handsome fellow," I said. Under normal circumstances I am not much enchanted by members of the canine species, but Humphrey had such a friendly way about him that I couldn't help but like him. He wagged his blunt tail so enthusiastically it made his chunky body shake all over.

"Here," she said, "I've got something for you."

She was carrying a copy of *Pride And Prejudice*, one of several Jane Austen novels I'd been forced at gunpoint to read in college. If you haven't encountered Miss Austen's work I wouldn't bother—it's mainly about women stuck out in the countryside pining away for this and that.

The girl said, "I run errands for Mr. Stewart. He asked me to give this to you if you came 'round."

Stuck in the book was an envelope, which young Freddy extracted and handed to me. My name was emblazoned on it.

I opened the envelope and read the note: "Dear Sir Errol. We have urgent business on the Continent and will return as soon as possible. In the meantime, please continue to apply your every effort to the task at hand. Madame C wishes you to know that it is more important now than ever."

So much for shoring up my faith! I must have let out an audible sigh of irritation, because young Freddy said, with concern in her voice, "Is everything all right, sir?"

"Oh, yes, Freddy. Nothing for you to worry about."

I expected her to be off back home, but she stayed beside me on the wall.

"With respect, sir, why do grown-ups always say that to children? When I ask my dad why he looks troubled he says the same thing. He tells me it's nothing for me to worry about. But if he's worried about something shouldn't I know about it, too?"

What a bright young lady! She reminded me a bit of myself at her age—always peppering the grown-ups with questions. "Well, Freddy, it's probably because your dad wants you to be carefree and not to be burdened by his worries."

She gave her head an irritated shake. She said, "But when he's troubled he ends up getting mad at me later on. I'm just trying to help by giving him someone to talk to about his troubles. He just keeps everything bottled up inside."

I scarcely knew what to say, not having had an actual conversation with a child since I was one myself at least twenty-five years ago. I felt as if I were getting a bit out of my depths, into territory best handled by her mother. I said, "That's very kind of you, Freddy. What does your mother say about all of that?"

"It's just Dad and me. My mother passed away when I was little."

"Oh, I'm so sorry, my dear. I lost my own mother when I could barely toddle."

"So you know what it's like. Did your father ever get married again?"

"So many times it made my head spin," I said.

She grinned and said, "You're funny, Sir Errol."

"So I've been told. You seem to have a bit of wit about you, too. Hang onto that, Freddy. One thing they can't take away from us is our ability to amuse ourselves."

It suddenly occurred to me that young Freddy might make a good detective's assistant.

I asked her, "Have you noticed any odd goings on around here?"

"Odd, sir? How?"

"Oh, the way people are behaving, that sort of thing."

"To be truthful, Sir Errol, everything always looks a bit odd to me."

"How so, Freddy?"

"It's the grown-ups, Sir Errol. I'm always trying to decide if it's the grown-ups who are crazy or if I'm the one who's crazy."

"My goodness, Freddy. Aren't you awfully young to be pondering thoughts like that?"

"Didn't you think about things like that when you were a young lad, Sir Errol?"

"Well, yes, I did. However, in the family I grew up in, there was no difficulty in identifying who the crazy ones were. Perhaps for survival, I became a keen student of their craziness at an early age. I also developed the ability to see exactly how they went out of their way to *make* themselves crazy."

"Tell me more, Sir Errol. This is what I am wondering, too."

"People make themselves crazy mostly by not telling the truth to each other or pretending they don't know the truth inside. They make themselves even crazier by punishing people who speak up and tell the truth."

I heard a sound that made my stomach tighten. Young Freddy was snuffling, with tears running down her face. My God! What is one supposed to do with a crying child? I noticed that my head was whipping back and forth, looking for someone to rescue me from this awkward situation. There was no one there. I was on my own.

I tried perking her up a bit. "I'm sure your father loves you very much," I said, but my utterance seemed to make things worse. She started sobbing outright, bringing a hot flush of shame that I had brought her injury. I said, "I'm so sorry to have upset you."

"No, no, it's all right. I feel the truth of what you are saying. I see the grown-ups do that all the time. They conceal their true feelings under many layers of artifice."

"And what's worse, my perceptive young friend, after a while they don't realize they're doing it. They get mad if you point it out to them. Have you gotten in trouble for telling the truth, Freddy?"

"Many times, Sir Errol. I said to my father, "Father, why are you so sad today?" and he said, "I'm not sad." But then later I discovered that it was the day he got married to my mother. Why couldn't he have just said, 'Thank you for noticing, Freddy. Today is my wedding anniversary and I'm feeling sad that your mother is not here."

I found myself warming to this articulate young lady. I had always gone out of my way to avoid children, particularly children of the adolescent variety. However, conversing with this curious young lady was making me begin to wonder if perhaps there might be some value to young people after all.

I said, "I don't wish to alarm you, Freddy, but you must be careful in your quest to penetrate the veil of artifice. Grown-ups, as you call them, have a very limited tolerance for reality. If you introduce too much of it at once they will snarl and snap at you."

I saw her head bobbing in agreement. She tilted her head up and gave me a brave smile. Her tears had stopped.

"So I have noticed, Sir Errol, but I had not been able to put those thoughts into words."

"You are doing quite well words-wise, my dear. I just want you to use your keen mind in ways that do not bring harm to you."

"What sort of harm should I fear?"

"Well, it wasn't so long ago that they were burning witches all across Europe."

She gave me a sharp look. "You have an unusual way of consoling those in sorrow, Sir Errol."

"So I've heard. Others have been kind enough to point that out to me."

Worry had replaced the sadness on her face. She said, "But shouldn't witches be burned, Sir Errol? Our pastor says that casting spells and such is evil."

"That's absurd, my dear. Witches were nothing more than herbalists and followers of their own special religions. Have you not noticed that all the priests and pastors and vicars are men? It got to be that way because they stamped out all the women who practiced their own religion. They called them witches and ran them out of business so they could have all the business for themselves. And believe me, dear Freddy, a very good business it is!"

"You have given me much to think about, Sir Errol, so much that I feel I must go home to digest it all."

"But wait, you haven't answered my question about odd goings-on."

She pursed her lips. "One thing—Lady Jennie has been much preoccupied of late."

"Lady Jennie?"

"She's the wife of the Lord who owns the estate but he's almost never home. She likes me to call her Jennie but I can't bring myself to do that so I call her Lady Jennie. She lets me borrow books from her and sometimes she likes me to read to her while she rests in the afternoon."

"And you say she has been preoccupied. Do you have a sense of what concerns her?"

"She has a son who is much involved with politics in London. I think she fears for his safety."

"She should worry more about his sanity," I said.

Freddy laughed out loud, and I found myself taking a bit of satisfaction that I had amused her, perhaps lightening the burden of being a keen, sensitive young lady enduring somewhat rough circumstances in life. Given her wit, though, I had faith she would triumph over all, providing of course she could keep to a minimum her reading of Jane Austen books.

I could see my young friend was eager to be off, so I wished her well and climbed back aboard the carriage for another molar-rattling journey back to the train station. When I returned to my flat I knocked on Francesca's door to ask if she might make me a restorative libation, which she was only too happy to do.

I changed into more comfortable clothes while she brewed the coffee, and then stretched out before the fireplace to warm myself up. When Francesca came in with the carafe I invited her to join me by the fire for a cup. She settled herself in a chair and poured our coffees.

She pointed to my notebook on the nearby table. "Have you been remembering to write down your dreams, Sir Errol?"

"To be honest, I forgot all about it, except for one sliver of a dream I caught this morning as I was waking."

"Oh! What was the dream?"

I picked up the notebook and flipped to the page. "There was a house fire, a young man running out with some art he rescued."

"That's very good, Sir Errol. You must try to grasp the meaning of it. My grandmother taught me a beautiful way to understand the meaning of dreams. Would you like me to show you?"

In spite of my urge to tell her that this whole dream business was a bunch of claptrap, I went along with her. "Very well," I said.

"You take each image from the dream and write it down. In your dream there were three main images: a house on fire, a running young man, and the rescue of art."

"I see. Then what do I do?"

"You consider each image as a part of yourself. You say, 'the house on fire is the part of me that's ___________.' You let your mind fill in the blank. Then you go on to the next image."

I wrote down the three images.

She said, "Now say 'the house of fire is the part of me that ___________.' "

"The house on fire is the part of me that ..." Nothing came to mind. I looked to Francesca for help.

"Just keep saying it. Sometimes it takes a few times."

"The house on fire is the part of me that..." Suddenly an idea came with a whoosh. "It's the part of me that needs to be destroyed to make room for something new."

Francesca clapped her hands. "That's wonderful, Sir Errol. Go on to the next one, 'the running man is the part of me that...' "

"The running man is the part of me that's... running out of time."

"Ah," she said, with a knowing nod. "You are such a dashing and energetic man that it makes one forget you are entering that phase of life called 'middle age.' "

"I liked the first part of your sentence a great deal more than the last part," I said, getting a chuckle out of Francesca.

She said, "Now do the one about rescuing the art."

"The art is the part of me that must be rescued at all cost."

"And what is the most valuable work of art in you, Sir Errol? What is the part of you that must be rescued at all cost?"

To my great surprise, sadness clutched my throat and tears stung my eyes. I felt a hot wave of embarrassment come over me at crying in front of Francesca. She must have sensed it, because she leaned over and patted my knee.

"It's all right, Sir Errol. Your tears are safe with me. Can you tell me what they are about?"

I felt the clutch of my throat release as I opened my mouth and said, "As I feel my body getting older I am afraid my mind will slow down, too. My curiosity has always served me well. I don't want to ever lose the part of me that wonders. I am afraid as I get older my wonder will go away and then where will I be?"

"Sir Errol, I am not yet at an age when I can fully appreciate what you are saying. I cannot tell you what lies ahead, but someday all of our faculties must come to an end. Someday you will say 'goodbye' to your wonder and curiosity, just as Leonardo had one day to bid farewell to the ability of his hand to draw pictures."

"My dear Francesca, you are so wise for such a young woman!"

"Thank you, Sir Errol, but we are not finished yet. What is that part of you that must be burned down to make room for something new? And what is the 'new' thing you are making room for?"

That stumped me. I had a vague sense of the answers but I could not put words on them. Suddenly I felt extremely in need of a good nap.

"I think I may have had enough excitement for one day, Francesca. Let me ponder your questions further when I am more refreshed."

She gave me a firm squeeze on the knee. "Yes, please rest. But remember, Sir Errol, these are not 'my' questions. These are 'your' questions. Your dreams are the vehicle for carrying wisdom from the depths of you to the surface."

I was getting so sleepy I could barely remain sitting upright. Francesca plumped up a pillow and encouraged me to stretch out on the divan. I felt a wave of gratitude suffuse me. "Thank you for your kindness, Francesca."

"You're very welcome, Sir Errol?"

I started to drift off and in that disembodied state heard myself murmuring, "I have always been blessed with magnificent women around me."

She smiled down at me and gave me a kiss on my forehead. "And why do you think that is, Sir Errol?"

"Grace and good fortune, I suppose."

"No doubt, but I think it's also because you appreciate us so lavishly."

On that happy note I rested my head on the pillow and surrendered myself to the welcome embrace of Morpheus.

CHAPTER THIRTEEN

When Tuesday rolled around I sent a message to Bratty to make sure he still wished to accompany me to the political gathering that evening. I held out the carrot that Francesca would be joining us. The courier brought a message right back from Bratty: "I am looking forward to it! Please ask Francesca to wear that silk dress again."

I sent the courier back with my reply: "I will certainly ask, but Francesca has a mind of her own. You know how women are with their garments. I don't want you to suffer needless pique if Francesca comes dressed in something else entirely."

I was turning to close the door when a taxicab clattered up in front of my flat. The carriage door flew open and out bounded a surprise visitor, perhaps the last person in the world I expected to drop in unannounced: Sherlock Holmes.

"Good morning, Holmes." I gave him a curt nod, indicating that he had some explaining to do.

He whipped off that ridiculous deerstalker cap he wears and gave me a tight little bow. "At your service, Sir Errol." He stepped forward and we shook hands.

What on earth was going on here? Instead of his usual attitude of looking down at me superciliously over the long, narrow and craggy reaches of his nose, he appeared to be paying obeisance to me. Unless my eyes were deceiving me, I was seeing a new version of Sherlock Holmes, one who appeared possibly to have a tiny speck of humility embedded in his depths.

I shook his hand and said, "I confess you have surprised me, Holmes. What has inspired you to call on me at such an early hour?"

"I have a unique proposition to discuss with you. May I come in?"

I took him inside and waited while he got out of his tweed cape. I watched him carefully hang the cape and the hat on the rack, and that is when I could contain myself no further.

"Good Lord, Holmes! How many times have I seen you out in public wearing that absurd hat? Please tell me—just what are you hoping to accomplish with that particular style of headwear? I've never seen a single person but you parading around London in a deerstalker hat! Perhaps you have not yet noticed, but in the city of London there are absolutely no deer on the loose!"

I paused to catch my wind, and that is when I saw something that got me completely undone: A tear was rolling down Holmes's cheek. The sudden gust of my utterance must have stirred some sort of sadness in him. I felt mortified that I had hurt his feelings, a condition I had previously thought to occur only in Jane Austen novels.

I said, "I'm sorry, dear chap. I meant no harm, but I see that my comments on your hat have hurt you."

He raised his hand to stop me. "No, it is not your fault. It's just that my deerstalker hat has sentimental attachment for me."

"Oh?"

"Yes. It was given me by a long-ago lady friend, a woman who touched me deeply and is no longer among the living."

"I'm so sorry."

He raised his hand again. "No need for apologies. The location of my sorrow is here in my own body. If you say something that stirs it, the responsibility lies entirely with me."

What an unusual distinction! I could see virtue in it, though. Much agitation goes on between people about who is responsible for what. As a child I remember being very puzzled when I heard my father yell at one of my stepmothers, "You're blaming me for that? I'm the one who ought to be blaming you!" The grown-ups could never seem to figure out whose fault anything was. Then later, when I heard him say virtually the same thing to a completely different stepmother, I began to wonder if it had anything to do with stepmothers at all.

"Now that we've got our pain located correctly, could I invite you to sit down for a drink?"

"Nothing of the alcoholic variety, thank you. However, if you were able to produce a cup of strong, black tea I might be inclined to drink it."

"I take that as a 'Yes'," I said. "And I believe I have the wherewithal to manufacture a cup of tea for you. Please come into the kitchen and tell me your proposition while I fix you up a cup."

I put on water to boil and tossed a generous three-finger pinch of Darjeeling into the pot.

He said, "It appears you are able to make do without a manservant or other household staff. Is that so?"

"Absolutely. I cannot bear the idea of someone hanging around all the time."

I decided not to mention my relationship with Francesca, the complexities of which would certainly elude an unsophisticated fellow such as Holmes.

"I admire the leanness of your operation, Hyde, but I could never get by on my own. I cannot cook a thing. In addition, I have a malady, something Dr. Freud would probably love to get his hands on. I am utterly revolted by even the thought of my hands touching dishwater."

I filed that fact away for future reference, but chose not to comment out loud. Instead I said, "While the water boils, would you care to tell more about this proposition of yours?"

"Indeed, Sir Errol. You and I have found ourselves at the same location on several separate occasions, both of us appearing to be engaged in activities of a detective nature. Are you familiar with the Rule Of Three, Sir Errol?"

I confessed my ignorance of this so-called rule.

He said, "If something happens one time you may rightfully regard it as happenstance. If a similar thing happens twice, it could still possibly be simple coincidence. However, if it happens a third time, you are witnessing a theme in development and are wise to ask yourself: Since I have been the common denominator in these three events, what is the lesson I need to learn here? For example, if a passing carriage splashes you once, simply curse the carriage and move on. If on the next street you get splashed again, you cannot be sure it's not just happenstance. But if a third cab splashes you on a different street, it is time to wonder if perhaps you are walking a bit too close to the curb. You and I have crossed paths twice of late, so before it happens for a third time I want to take the reins of destiny into my own hands."

"Precisely what destiny are we seizing the reins of, Holmes?"

"Please call me Sherlock."

"All right, Sherlock it is, then. I confess you've got me a bit scrambled with all this talk about destiny. You are not the first person to bring destiny into the conversation of late."

"You are speaking, no doubt, of Madame C," he said, rendering me speechless for a moment.

When I recovered I said, "Yes, in fact I was. It would seem that Madame C is also among your circle of acquaintances."

"Indeed. I first cast my eye on the good lady a year or so ago, along with her cohorts, Malcolm Stewart and Freda. However, they are merely peripheral to the line of detection I am pursuing."

I peeked into the teapot and approved of its dark hue. I poured Sherlock a cup and watched while he took a sip.

"Excellent," he said.

"I'm glad you like it. I must always add a generous amount of sugar to make tea palatable."

"Not I," he said. "I find that the intense concentration of tannin matches a certain quality of bitterness that resides near the center of me."

I was somewhat taken aback by the intimate nature of his confession, but I did not find it completely off-putting. In fact, I found myself wondering: Is he trying to make friends with me? That idea would have seemed laughable to me an hour earlier.

Emboldened by his revelation of inner bitterness, I mused out loud: "Perhaps that is why the English are so devoted to their tea. I wonder if an overconsumption of tannins accounts for the bitter and mordant nature of English wit."

He chuckled and said, "I don't know, but it certainly accounts for the dismal coloration of our teeth."

I couldn't help but join him in his chuckle. He was ever so right. On the rare occasions when English people bare their teeth in a smile, it looks as warm and inviting as Stonehenge by moonlight.

I said, "Now that we have exhausted the conversational possibilities of bitter beverages, please enlighten me as to the central purpose of your visit."

"Indeed," he said. "Here it is: let us pool our information. I shall tell you what I am exploring and you do the same with me."

"My goodness, Sherlock! You are widely regarded as a 'lone wolf' in your pursuits. I'm surprised that you would considering sharing information with anyone, least of all a fellow detective."

"Times change, dear fellow. Yes, even people change, although a cursory glance at the great mass of humanity might lead one to think otherwise."

"I am not opposed to your idea, but I can see certain practical problems. As you know, I am writing a book on my adventures. Would it not bother you to play only a "bit part," as the theater folk say? In the stories about you, you are always the star of the show."

"I would be honored to play even the tiniest part in your tome, Sir Errol. Thanks to Dr. Watson, and over my most strenuous objections, I find myself regarded as something of a mythical superhero by the general public. And as you well know, there is nothing of heroic virtue about the pursuits of a detective. It is merely applying elementary logic in an orderly fashion. The fact that almost no human being is willing to take the time to do this makes us appear mysterious and god-like to them."

Here, in all its glory, was the famous arrogance of Sherlock Holmes! From the lofty, Olympian perch atop his superior intellect he could look down on the rest of humanity and pronounce them unfit. Come to think of it, though, he made a very good point. Private detectives, and of course the people who read about their exploits, are without doubt the crowning glory of human evolution.

Sherlock interrupted my thoughts: "You have no doubt given much consideration to the art of detection, Sir Errol. How do you describe our noble profession?"

"I call it the art of bumbling about with curious intent. If people only knew how little romance there is in our profession! In my experience, detection is 99% plod and 1% panic."

He slapped his thigh and laughed out loud. "That's very good—very good, indeed. What we do in those moments of panic is important, but the great preponderance of our work is taking pains not only to look but to *see.*"

"I couldn't agree more."

"Excellent. Now, may I provide you a bit more detail on how we might benefit from sharing information?"

"Very well," I said, injecting a hint of reluctance into my voice to let him know I wasn't some sort of pushover.

"You must certainly recall the fellow at Mr. Poindexter's dinner party who wore the lavender beret."

"Of course, although at the moment I can't call up his name."

"His name is Dietrich Eckart."

"Ah, yes, he was visiting from Germany with those two odd young men."

"Precisely. I have taken a keen interest in Herr Eckart over the past year, and the more I learn about him the more pressing my concern becomes. I believe him to be engaged in pursuits most nefarious."

Suddenly a bolt of awareness shot through me: Was Eckart the bald devil of whom Madame C spoke? I had not seen him without his beret, but one could easily imagine that it concealed a hairless head.

"The color leaves your face, Sir Errol. Have you seen a ghost?"

"Perhaps I have. Madame C spoke most passionately about a 'bald devil' that I must do everything to stop. Could I have been seated at table with this very devil of hers?"

"I do not concern myself with 'devils' or 'angels' or any such otherworldly nonsense. All I can tell you is that Dietrich Eckart is that most dangerous of all the animals: a very smart human with very bad ideas."

"Such as?"

"Eckart envisions a continent, including the British Isles, organized and administered by the Germans. He wishes to cleanse Europe of all forms of humanity he considers unsuitable, mainly the Jews."

"Good God, no! That would be wretchedly inconvenient! Both my accountant and my internist are Jews."

"I am glad that the subject touches you on such a deep and personal level," Sherlock said.

Did I detect a trace of irony in his voice? Before I could dwell on that question he surged onward. "Eckart would not only eliminate all the Jews from Europe but also gypsies, communists and homosexuals."

"Really? Where would we get our theater?"

"Quite," said Holmes. "Sir Errol, may I ask you if you happen to play the ancient and venerable game of chess?"

"No. Not since childhood, anyway. Why do you ask?"

"Dietrich Eckart is a fanatical enthusiast of the game. I don't think it would be too much of an exaggeration to say that he sees the whole world as a chessboard. You recall, no doubt, the pale young man accompanying Eckart at Mr. Poindexter's party."

"Yes. What of him?"

"He is a Russian chess prodigy, a 15-year-old who already astonishes the old masters of the game with the brilliance of his play, which is said to be relentless and utterly without mercy. Eckart brought him from Moscow, ostensibly to play several of the top European players, but I suspect there is a furtive and much more malevolent purpose to the enterprise."

"What sort of purpose?"

"That, my esteemed colleague, is the question I am most keenly eager to answer. Did you notice the eyes on Herr Eckart's other young companion, the so-called artist?"

"I did not notice his eyes, but he gave the overall impression of great agitation. What of his eyes?"

"I had seen those eyes before only on religious fanatics and political fanatics, but from my brief conversations with the young artist I could discern no spiritual impulses. I can only fathom that he must be a political fanatic under the guise of an artist."

"I didn't quite catch his last name when we were introduced. Did you?"

"Yes. Hitler, with one 't.' "

"And the young chess prodigy?"

"His name was Alexander Alekhine."

"I must say, Sherlock, you are a whiz with names. I'm awful with them."

"Thank you, Sir Errol. It is a small point of pride with me. I employ a trick to remember names. When I am introduced to people I quickly say their name three times in my mind. For some reason it makes the name stick."

"Most masterful. I should adopt the technique myself, but I'm quite sure I'm not capable of the mental gymnastics required to say 'Alexander Alekhine' even twice, let alone three times."

"I'm sure you underestimate yourself, Sir Errol. In fact, if I may be permitted an observation at such an early stage of our personal relationship, you are a very puzzling combination of qualities."

"How so, Holmes?"

"I thought we had agreed upon 'Sherlock'?"

"Very well, Sherlock. What are these qualities of mine you find so puzzling to contemplate?"

"With respect, Sir Errol, one moment you radiate mastery and self-confidence, but then a few moments later you can appear to be completely oblivious. Is this a deliberate act you perform, to mask your underlying genius, or are you actually handicapped at times in your ability to see the perfectly obvious?"

The bloody cheek of this man! However, I managed to contain my outrage and simply said, "Your observation jostles me slightly, but I cannot say I'm reeling from it. My former fiancée, Lady Forsythia Highgate, has on more than one occasion used that very word, 'oblivious,' in conversations about my shortcomings. However, I had previously assumed her criticisms were largely due to hormonal fluctuations."

"Perhaps a second look would be in order."

"Perhaps, but then again, one could argue that we should leave those things alone. As a great American poet says, 'Do I contradict myself? Very well, then I contradict myself. I am large, I contain multitudes.' "

"That's quite remarkable. Who wrote that?"

"Walt Whitman," I said.

"Walt who?"

Unable to resist giving him a tweak, I said, "Whitman. Just say it three times in your head."

That trimmed his sails a bit and he got back to the business at hand.

He said, "Now to the pressing matter. One of the urchins I employ keeps an eye on Victoria Station for me. He is quite certain he spotted Eckart's two young men, Hitler and Alekhine, boarding a train to Dover. We can hazard a guess that they were returning to the Continent."

"But Herr Eckart was not with them?"

"He was not observed, but that does not mean he wasn't there. My Irregulars are not perfect in their observational skills."

"Very well. What are you proposing we do?"

"One of us must follow the two young men; the other must stay here, in case Herr Eckart did not accompany Hitler and Alekhine to the Continent."

"That seals it then. There's no way I'm going to go careening about Europe in search of God knows what. My need for foreign travel is at an especially low ebb, virtually indistinguishable from none whatsoever."

"I did not know you had such strong feelings on the subject. In that case, I am bound for the Continent posthaste. You must be on the lookout for Eckart. There is a very real possibility that he did not accompany his two young charges and is up to some mischief here." He shot out his hand to shake mine, and then bounded down the steps toward his carriage. Before he got into the cab he turned and called to me. "In dire circumstances, Sir Errol, what do you use as a weapon?"

"A single-shot Derringer, but in all honesty, I've never had the occasion to fire it in hostility."

"I suggest you take some practice, then. That tiny firearm was designed to shoot a person sitting across from you at a card table. Beyond that range you must rely on prayer and hope that your bullet finds its mark."

I attempted a small jest, saying, "If our Eckart really is a devil, bullets may not work, anyway." Sherlock, however, did not seem to apprehend the humor in my remark.

He gave his head an impatient shake. "As I said, there are no 'devils' in the world, only smart people with terrible ideas."

"Well, then, if I meet Dietrich Eckart again I shall attempt to put some better ideas into his head."

"I wish you the very best luck with that. However, rather than putting better ideas in his head I would be content to have you put a bullet in it."

I don't mind telling you I was a bit rattled after Holmes left, so I consulted my hashish pipe a bit earlier in the day than usual. Afterwards, when serenity had replaced the butterflies my conversation with Sherlock had stirred up, I decided to take his advice and do a little practicing with my Derringer. I called down to Francesca to warn her that I was about to make some noise, but then remembered she had classes all day. She had promised me she would be home in plenty of time to dress for our excursion with Bratty to the political gathering.

I took the pistol down to the basement and pulled an old mattress up against the wall. I ripped a page out of a magazine and taped it in the center of the mattress. It happened to be a Scottish innkeeper's special recipe for haggis. How fitting, I thought: a long-overdue chance to express my resentment at being coerced into trying a few bites of haggis during a childhood visit to Scotland with my father and a new stepmother.

I loaded up the pistol and stepped back from the target a couple of yards, to the across-the-card-table distance mentioned by Holmes. I aimed and fired off a loud POP, blowing a satisfying hole near the center of the haggis recipe. With the barrel still warm in my hand, I loaded it again and stepped back three more paces to approximately twenty feet away from the target. I took aim and fired; this time I missed the target by a good foot, leaving a smoking hole in the mattress.

It occurred to me that another puff or two off the hashish pipe might steady my hand and improve my aim. After a short break to fortify myself thusly, I loaded the pistol again and took aim: POP! This time, unfortunately, I missed the mattress completely, blowing a hole in the wall above it. From this modest experiment I concluded that hashish might not be the best facilitator of good marksmanship. I cleaned the pistol and put it away, making a mental note to avoid the use of firearms unless I found myself in the direst of circumstances.

By then it was time to bathe and dress for the evening. I was putting the finishing touches on my tuxedo when Francesca knocked on my door. She had gotten my note about Bratty's request and was clad magnificently in his favorite clingy dress, accessorized by a simple strand of pearls and a gray suede clutch.

I had a last-moment inspiration for my own outfit, but I decided to consult Francesca about it before I took the bold step of implementing it.

"Do you think it would look good if I wore this red cashmere scarf about my neck tonight?"

"Sir Errol! I think it would look splendid! Usually you do not concern yourself much with these sorts of fashion touches. Where did you get such a radical notion?"

"Remember that dancer-person at Bratty's dinner party? Isadora? She was wearing a scarf around her neck indoors and I thought it looked rather fetching. Also, my neck tends to get cold even indoors on these damp evenings."

"I give it a strong 'YES'!" Francesca said, and thus we stepped out into our evening.

After a bit of the old prance-and-clatter we got over to Bratty's place, where he was waiting for us on the front steps. When Bratty climbed into the carriage, resplendent in a beautifully cut tuxedo, his eyes went wide with approval. "Francesca, you look utterly ravishing tonight!" She rewarded him with a generous flutter of eyelash and a bashful dip of the head. His tore his eyes away from Francesca and glanced over at me, "And oh yes—Hullo, Errol."

. . .

My mood was chipper when I arrived at the political gathering, but after about twenty minutes I became radiantly aware, once again, of why I loathe political gatherings. The men were wearing standard evening attire—that is to say we all looked like stuffed penguins—while the ladies were got up in gowns and bejeweled to the gills. People were milling about the room, pumping each other's hands and issuing forth great gusts of forced laughter. If being fatuous was an art form we were a roomful of Rembrandts.

I quickly lost enthusiasm for squiring Bratty and Francesca through the throngs of people in the room, so I set them off on their own and retreated in a mild sulk to the bar. Sadly, there was no balm for my mood to be found there, either. The only beverage being dispensed was champagne, a drink I regard as only slightly preferable in taste to medicinal mouthwash.

Fortunately I had taken care earlier to build a base of conviviality for the evening, in the form of a lungful or two from my precious hoard of hashish from the Kulu Valley of India. The Kulu Valley product is highly valued by connoisseurs because of its spiritual effects, said to derive from the manner in which it is created. Come harvest season, naked young virgins from the village dance and writhe their way through the plants by moonlight, accompanying themselves with finger-cymbals and ankle-bells, allowing the precious resins to cling to their bodies. Then, a team comprised of the clan's womenfolk scrape off the resins, using the large leaf of the local Deodar cedar. Finally, men of the village are called in to form the resin into chunks of various weights and transport it to market. I've heard it said that the profits from a single pound of Kulu Valley hashish can feed a family for a year.

In my own modest attempt to lift up the lives of those less fortunate than myself, I had purchased a pound of their finest a year or so ago myself from a Punjabi rug merchant of my acquaintance. In addition to savoring the spiritual benefits of the hashish I am also able to enjoy the heartwarming satisfactions of philanthropy.

I was standing near the bar, sipping a mineral water and finding amusement in watching English people trying to dance, when I caught sight of a rather fetching young woman also observing the dancers. The orchestra was playing a slow waltz, one of the three dance steps I can manage, so I sidled over to her, introduced myself and proposed that we take a turn about the floor.

She said, "I would be delighted, Mr. Hyde," but beneath her cordial tone I thought I detected an edge of anger.

"And how may I address you, dear lady?"

"My name is Clementine, but you may call me Clemmie," she said.

We began our slow sway about the room, but within the first minute or so I could feel that young Clemmie was only a reluctant participant. Although she gave me a couple of smiles it appeared that her attention was focused more on activities over my shoulder. Finally she drew to a halt and led me off the dance floor.

"I'm so sorry," she said, "but I believe I agreed to dance with you under false pretenses."

I was a bit nonplussed by her utterance. "I don't understand."

She sighed and told me that her attention was on the young man she had come with, who was now out on the dance floor with a rival for his affections. She said, "We have gone back and forth for more than a year about whether we are engaged or not."

My goodness! I had inadvertently waltzed my way into a lover's quarrel. I followed her gaze across the dance floor and saw the young man in question, gliding about the floor with a woman who appeared to be at least five years his senior.

Attempting to help elevate young Clemmie's mood I said, "She looks a tad old for him."

Her eyes flew open wide, but she didn't chide me for the boldness of my observation. Instead she said, "I think that's part of his fascination with her. He's a bit of a mama's boy."

This was all getting a bit too deep for me, so I said, "I must toddle off now. I need to make sure my guests aren't getting lonely. I wish you well with your gentleman."

She gave me a brave smile and shook my hand. "I'm sure it will all get sorted out," she said.

Whew! I set off in search of Francesca and Bratty, making a firm resolve to attempt no further excursions onto the dance floor. It brought to mind Grandmother Hyde's oft-stated warning, one which I had not heeded particularly well, "Avoid dancing, Errol—one never knows what forces may be unleashed." She had met my grandfather on the dance floor, and there is no need to remind anyone what came of that.

I caught up with my guests, deep in conversation with a clutch of grim-faced political folk. They were earnestly discussing something terrible that was happening on the Continent, but since something terrible was always going on over there it didn't hold much interest for me.

I spotted Darcy Slatkin across the room talking to a gaggle of people and decided to take my conversational chances with him.

Darcy saw me coming and stepped over to greet me.

"I'm glad you made it, Errol. Did you bring your friends?"

"Indeed. They're over there, discussing deep things with a crew of somber politicians."

"You are such a cynic, Errol. Perhaps this evening will cheer you up a bit about the world of politics."

So far I was not feeling the cheer. "I say, Darcy, is this the whole thing? Does everyone just stand around and talk until they get too drunk to function? Or is there some purpose to our gathering?"

"Oh, yes, there is definitely a purpose! In fact, very shortly several of our most promising young public servants will be giving brief speeches. We are entering a new era of British politics, Errol! It is most exciting. Mark my words, there are young people in this room who possess the talents to serve the Crown as ambassadors, ministers, even prime ministers!"

Almost on cue, a cheer broke out across the room near the stage, welcoming one of the young politicians up to speak. The crowd fell silent as he began to wax eloquent, quite obviously in love with the sound of his voice. Fortunately I was spared having to listen by a pressing need to visit the toilet. I wasn't sure whether the young politician's utterances were to blame for my sudden urge, but I couldn't help noticing the coincidence.

When I returned from the gentlemen's washroom I felt about five pounds lighter and in no mood to burden myself with more political hooey. I noted that a new speaker was giving forth on the podium; upon closer inspection I saw it was Clemmie's wayward boyfriend. I scanned the crowd for signs of Clemmie and caught sight of her scurrying toward the exit clutching her coat. It appeared that the lovers' spat had not been resolved.

Truth be told, I was bored stiff. I decided to find my guests and let them know I'd had my fill. I set off around the periphery of the crowd to look for them but suddenly I saw something that made a chill run up my spine: Was that Dietrich Eckart tucked into a corner observing the proceedings? It was too dim to see for sure, but the tall figure looked very much like the "bald devil" himself, minus the beret. He was partially obscured by a curtain and his face was in shadows, but I could see the top of his bullet-domed pate glinting in the weak light.

I hurried through the throng to get a better look but by the time I'd navigated the crowd he had disappeared! I could still see the curtain swaying next to where he had been standing. Thinking he'd ducked behind it I ran to the corner and peered through but saw nothing except a blank wall. It was as if he had simply vaporized. A peculiar scent hung in the air, somewhat like the metallic tinge one smells just before a thunderstorm. It jogged a scent-memory in me; I realized I had caught whiffs of the same smell sitting across the dinner table from Eckart at Bratty's ill-fated dinner party.

Applause erupted behind me and I turned to see Clemmie's beau taking a bow from the stage. I decided to check with the doormen outside to find out if they had seen Eckart leave. As I hurried toward the exit I heard the master of ceremonies announce the next speaker. Before I could get to the door, however, Darcy Slatkin bustled over and blocked my egress.

"Surely you can't be leaving, Sir Errol! The evening has just gotten underway in earnest."

"I offer you my humblest apologies, Darcy, but it's the 'earnest' part that makes my skin crawl. I must check with my doctor; I may have an actual, medically-certifiable allergy to earnestness."

Darcy huffed and puffed and turned a bit pink before he responded. "But, Errol, society has many serious problems! How else will they be solved but through the earnest activities of politicians?"

"With all due respect, my dear Darcy, it seems to me that a good many of society's problems are *caused* by earnest politicians."

"Whatever do you mean?"

"I seem to recall that our government spends hundreds of thousands of pounds every year to improve the lives of poor people."

"Yes, of course. That is one thing governments are supposed to do."

"If you say so. But have you not noticed that the more money the government spends on alleviating poverty, the greater the number of poor people there are in the world?"

He began to sputter and cough, no doubt moved by the powerful force of my insight.

I sailed on, "While we are on the subject, I read recently that the Chancellor of the Exchequer, whose name I'm not recalling at the moment—"

"David Lloyd George," Darcy hissed, a bit testily I thought.

"Yes, of course. This Lloyd George fellow seemed to be saying he was going to jack up taxes on the wealthy to pay for all sorts of benefits for the poor. Did I understand that correctly?"

"Yes, and if you had been listening a few minutes ago you would have heard one of Lloyd George's brightest young supporters receive abundant applause for his platform."

"Now we're getting to my point, Darcy! You are vastly wealthy, as are many people in the room. Why would rich people clap for someone who boldly proclaims that he intends to fleece them?"

I watched Darcy's dream of converting me to his cause sink slowly from his face. Before he could slink away, though, I asked him if he had seen a tall, bald fellow at the gathering.

"Are you serious? This room is rife with tall, bald men."

"The one I'm talking about has a special scent about him."

Darcy grimaced. "You must mean that German fellow, Eckart. It must be some cologne he wears."

"That's exactly who I mean. So he was here tonight. Do you know who invited him?"

"Yes, I believe he is a guest of one of the gentlemen who will speak later this evening." Again I saw the bitter downturn of his mouth.

I said, "It appears you don't like that particular speaker."

"I do not. He represents the extreme right wing of our political spectrum, one of those fellows who thinks the Magna Carta was far too liberal a document when it did away with the divine right of kings. Why are you so interested in Eckart, anyway?"

"It's complicated," I said, "But could you perhaps draw on your connections to arrange an introduction to him?"

"I might be able to do better than that. A few of the best and brightest assembled here tonight are going to be staying out in Burley next weekend. I'm going out myself, and I understand Eckart will be there also. Perhaps you might be interested in joining us."

I tried to picture myself spending an entire weekend in Burley trapped in a house full of political types; it brought an unpleasant taste of bile to the back of my throat. I said, "It's a generous offer, Darcy, but I wouldn't dream of imposing upon your hospitality. How about if I simply get a hotel room nearby and come over for dinner and a chat?"

"Fine. I'll let the host know and send you all the details."

After I detached myself from Darcy I ventured outside to ask the doormen and footmen if they had seen Eckart leave. I received the same answer from everyone: "No, sir." I was not surprised. You wouldn't expect the devil to leave through the front door.

I climbed into a motorized taxi and bid the cabbie to take me home. Within the hour I was pajama-clad and tucked up in my bed, savoring a cup of hot chocolate, with my well-worn copy of Epictetus' *Enchiridion* at hand.

As I sipped my cocoa I let my tired eyes wander over his opening lines:

The secret of happiness is this: know that some things you can control and some things you cannot.

I was eternally grateful to my old philosophy tutor at Cambridge, Godfrey Rumbottom, for introducing me to Epictetus. When I graduated he gifted me with his own copy of the *Enchiridion*, the one I was holding in my hand.

"Remember, Errol," Old Godfrey said, "any time you come up against an obstacle in your life, just open the *Enchiridion* and read the first page. You can work out any problem by discerning between that which you actually can change and that which is completely outside your power to change. You will no doubt discover, as I have, that 99% of everything in life is in the Cannot Change category. Learn to base your actions on the 1% you actually have control over and all will be well."

It was darn fine advice, even if it did come from an old reprobate who, once he had a few gin-and-tonics in him, would deviate slightly from the course of pure philosophy by proposing to any undergraduates within range that he bugger them forthwith. Protecting the sanctity of my nether regions has always been one of my very highest priorities. To that end, so to speak, I had successfully fended my tutor off on more than one occasion by giving him a sharp nudge with my elbow, an instrument that definitely fits in my Can Control category. Fortunately, when he sobered up he never held any grudges against his pupils for rejecting him.

Later, as I nestled my head on my favorite pillow to drift into sleep, a long-forgotten memory passed through my mind. When I was a little boy my grandmother was often in charge of seeing to my daily nap. Once she could finally corral me into taking a nap, she would get me settled on the bed and tell me a story. The stories always ended with a special practice my grandmother believed to be salubrious in inducing sweet dreams. She would ask me to tell her all the things for which I felt grateful. I would always spend my last few moments of wakefulness in a state of gratitude.

The memory flushed the elusive rabbit of happiness from its burrow deep within me and sent it sprinting through my body. In that spacious state of near-dreamy consciousness just before I fell into slumber I floated items of gratitude through my mind: for my life itself and the luxuries I was able to surround myself with, for my friends and acquaintances—the whole strange and lively bunch of them—and for the gift of curiosity itself, my mainstay as I bumble about in the business of my earthly sojourn.

I sent off a telepathic note of appreciation to my grandmother, another to the mother I hardly knew, and even one to my father with all his faults and flaws. The last image I remember before falling asleep was being at the Tivoli gardens in Copenhagen when I was a little boy, on one of Father's bachelor vacations, getting to ride the Ferris wheel over and over by myself while Father stayed below, chatting up the big, buxom Danish girl who sold the tickets. Round and round went the wheel until I slipped into the arms of sweet Morpheus.

CHAPTER FOURTEEN

I don't know if it was the pre-sleep recital of gratitude that did the trick, but that night I had the most remarkable and vivid dream of my life. I was in a vast landscape, a field of all possibilities spread out before me like an infinite array of delights to be sampled. In the dream I discovered I could take flight by a slight shift of my mind. I was leaping along the ground in long, extended steps and then in the next moment I realized I could fly if I lightened up in my mind, like letting go of whatever limitations bound me. On the next leap I stayed airborne! Then I discovered something even better: if I kept lightening up and letting go, by simply dismissing anything I thought limited me, I soared effortlessly up into the air as far as I wanted to go!

I swooped and soared above the landscape a quarter-mile or so in the air, enjoying the twisting and turning of free flight. I had hardly begun to revel in the new sensation when another part of my mind began to wonder why I was suddenly able to fly. As soon as I had the "Why?" thought I started losing altitude and felt a wave of panic that I was going to make a crash landing. Before I hit the ground, though, I realized that asking "Why?" might be what was weighting me down, so instead of asking why I could fly, I let go of "Why?" and simply relaxed into the mystery of it all. Immediately I gained altitude again and resumed my soaring swoops and turns. I continued to feel the sweet sensation of being gravity free as I woke up and gave myself a deep morning stretch.

I could hardly wait for Francesca to come up with my morning coffee so I could tell her the dream. After I did so, she exclaimed, "Sir Errol, what a wonderful dream! You can mine its riches forever."

"Really? What do you see in it?"

She laughed and said, "You're not going to get away with that, Sir Errol. The question is what do YOU see in it?"

"I hardly know what to say. I suppose the main thing is that I accomplished my feat by letting go of any pre-conceived notion of what could happen, by simply dismissing any notion that I was limited by what I had taken for granted before."

"You said 'lightening up.' "

"Yes, that's what it felt like."

"I can't think of any part of life that wouldn't be made better by lightening up. People are far too grave, don't you think?"

"I couldn't agree more."

"Your detective activities might also benefit from the life lesson your dream gave you."

"How do you mean?"

"As a detective you're always trying to find out 'why' something happened or 'why' somebody did something, are you not?"

"Yes, of course."

"Well, then, there you have it: when you come to a dead end asking 'why,' simply let go, lighten up and enjoy the mystery of it all."

"Hmmm, I'm not sure my clients would pay me if I said, 'I didn't solve your problem, but I enjoyed the mystery of it all.' "

"I don't think it would come to that. I would bet that if you lightened up and let go of the 'why' and the 'how' and the 'who' for a moment, you would perhaps dip into a deeper and more creative level of the mind."

"My goodness, Francesca, I had no idea you were such a fount of wisdom in this area."

"Then now is the perfect time to tell you of a decision I have come to. When I finish my legal secretary studies next month I want to prepare myself to attend medical school, on my way to becoming a psychoanalyst."

"Good God, Francesca! Surely you must see the folly in that scheme!"

"You no doubt are going to recite a list of limitations such as the fact that almost never do any of the medical schools admit women."

"Yes, of course. I would be derelict in my duties as your guardian of sorts if I did not point that out."

"And you would no doubt bring up the possible loss of the affections of Mr. Poindexter and the easy life I would have as Mrs. Poindexter."

"That, too," I said. However, a most unfamiliar feeling was beginning to creep over me. I tried to think of a better word for it, but I finally had to admit that it could only be described as "sheepish."

Francesca gave me a big smile. "The look on your face tells me the truth might be dawning on you."

"Yes, I believe it is. All those limitations we just recited are barriers simply because we think they are."

"Yes, and your dream gave us the solution. All I need to do is let go of whatever I think my limitations are and let some deeper part of my mind come up with a solution."

As soon as she said that, a flurry of ideas started popping off in my mind. Perhaps there weren't as many barriers as we thought. For one thing, I could easily pay for her tuition by forgoing a few pairs of bespoke shoes each year. It would be a dreadful sacrifice, of course, but perhaps also character-building. There was also the possibility of appealing to Bratty's better angels in hopes he might contribute to the project. I had a hunch that after he threw a tantrum or two, Bratty might calm down and see the long-term value of having a gorgeous partner who was also happy, fulfilled and grateful. It was a singularly rare combination of qualities, such that I had personally not observed any examples of it in my travels, but that didn't mean it wasn't possible.

"I think it's already working, Francesca! I've got your medical education paid for already."

"Please explain!"

And so I did, bringing the girl to tears, but of the good kind.

. . .

I seem to remember the Old Bard saying something about life creeping by a petty pace. He must have been clogged up by stodgy food when he wrote that line. Later, when he obtained relief, he probably cranked out snappier lines like "Cry 'Havoc!' And let slip the dogs of war."

My life definitely didn't creep by at a petty pace the week before I left for the country. Indeed, it went by in a bit of a whirl, partly because another case dropped into my lap the day after the political gathering.

A woman consulted me to help her determine if her husband was having an affair. Normally I do not engage with such issues, finding them a bit tawdry for my taste, but in this case I immediately agreed to assist her. I had a personal reason: Her husband was a pillar of society, greatly respected for his piety and good works, and almost nothing in the realm of amusement gives me more pleasure than to snatch up a hypocrite by the nape of his nefarious neck and hold him up to ridicule.

Any experienced detective will tell you the same thing: If you suspect your husband is having an affair, nine times out of ten you're right. He is indeed having an affair. In fact, by the time a wife gets around to suspecting her mate is on the stray, he's probably already racked up multiple affairs. (Dear Readers, if you find my assessment of husbands a bit harsh I can only say: spend a few years in the detective trade and I bet you will agree with me. In my earlier days as a detective, suspicious wives sought my services on the average of twice a week. After a year or so of hearing their stories I began to wonder if the hallowed institution of marital fidelity was largely a myth. I did a bit of research on the subject and found a relevant tidbit: a publication from back in the 18th century declared that, of the 874,000 married couples in England, only nine were happy. Just how they determined that number was a mystery they didn't disclose, but I didn't find it overly pessimistic. As far as I could see, things hadn't improved much; in my forty years of earthly sojourn I hadn't encountered even one happily married couple, let alone nine.)

I was able to wrap up the case in two days of shadowing the wayward husband. It turned out he was not only cheating on his wife with a saucy lass who worked in an East End pub, he was also seeing a third woman behind the bargirl's back. I felt like calling him aside and giving him a good talking-to. As I had learned through unpleasant personal experience, if you find yourself cheating on your mistress, your life has gotten just a bit too complicated.

I was finally able to catch him *flagrante delicto* by trailing him to a tiny apartment in Soho. The door was marked with a little card: Mildred Puth, Piano Lessons By Appointment.

Using my trusty keyhole lens I took a look at Mildred's inner sanctum and saw the good gentleman sprawled back on a sofa, still wearing his jacket, tie and vest but with his pants pooled down around his ankles. The piano teacher's head was bobbing rhythmically, performing a different style of music on a solo instrument, one that required not only nimble fingers but also a firm *embouchure.*

I put my lens away and politely waited until she brought the business to completion before knocking softly at the door. No need to ruin a fellow's entire day. Moments later Mildred opened the door and peered out with a quizzical look, dabbing daintily at her lips with a handkerchief. I smiled and opened my palm to her, revealing a gold sovereign. Her eyes popped with astonishment as I slipped it into her hand and said, "May I come in?"

I stepped into the room and saw our pillar of society hopping about on one foot, struggling to get his other leg into his pants.

I waited until he got his britches pulled up and said, "Good day, Mr. Asquith. I bring you greetings from the Mrs."

I expected him to sputter with outrage and demand that I get off the premises, but he surprised me by collapsing back down on the sofa and bursting into tears. I don't mind telling you, it took the edge right off the pleasure I was deriving from the moment. As I stood there, mouth hanging agape, I flashed back in my mind to the moment I waxed sarcastic on Sherlock's deerstalker hat. He had shed tears, shaking me up a bit, and now I was getting the same sort of reaction from a captured miscreant. It made me wonder if there was some kind of theme developing. Would total strangers soon be lurching up to me on the street to collapse sobbing on my shoulder? Perhaps I should start wearing a cape, as Sherlock does, in order to better protect myself against such unhygienic encounters.

"Now, now, Mr. Asquith, I know you'll soon see the brighter side of all this."

He blinked at me through his tears and said, "What brighter side is there?"

"Once a secret is out you are free from the burden of carrying it around. Any embarrassment you feel at being found out is far outweighed by the relief you feel after you make your confession."

"You don't know my wife," he said. "She is not likely to take kindly to my confession."

"Nonsense," I said. "Your wife seems like a perfectly reasonable person to me. And besides, wives almost always prefer knowing the truth over being lied to."

"Really?"

"Absolutely. And the ones who prefer being lied to aren't worth being married to."

"Gadzooks! What an unusual point of view!"

"Then I will take the liberty of going to even further extremes," I said. "Since you don't seem to find your wife a scintillating companion, why don't you simply take up residence elsewhere? Divorce is not common but on the other hand it is not the disgrace it once was. My own father did it any number of times."

Mr. Asquith groaned, "I would have to leave half my fortune behind, as well as my beloved rat terrier. My wife would never let go of the dog."

"So let me understand. You are living in a miserable situation so you won't have to lose half of it?"

That sobered him up even further. He said, "I hadn't looked at it quite that way."

"It might be wise to do so. A quick glance at the distinguished amount of grey and white in your hair would suggest that you are no longer in the first bloom of youth."

"I'm sixty."

"Very well, then. You know the old saying about the human lifespan: three score and ten years. So let's say you've got another ten good years in you, providing you don't get run over by one of those new buses that are beginning to lumber about London. Wouldn't it be better to take the short-term pain in favor getting a decade of freedom?"

Rather than answering my question he changed the subject on me. He said, "Tell me, how much is my wife paying you for your services?"

"Nothing so far. I often leave it up to my client to choose an amount that reflects the value they receive. From past experience, I would guess that it would be worth at least a hundred pounds to her."

"She is known for her generosity. However, what if I gave you two hundred pounds to forget this whole business and give her a clean report on me?"

"You disappoint me, Mr. Asquith, and I rebuke your suggestion most strenuously. First, you presume me to be a man who is open to negotiation on matters of integrity, and I am not such a man. Second, please note that you are willing to spend two hundred pounds so that you can continue to live a life that is making you miserable!"

He stared glumly at the carpet for a moment, shaking his head from side to side. I decided it would be a humane gesture to throw him a life preserver.

"Out of the goodness of my heart I am willing to postpone my report to your wife until Monday, as I am leaving for the country this afternoon. By Monday, I expect you to make a full confession to your wife and to develop two separate plans: one for staying and one for leaving, depending on your wife's preferences and your own."

"Two days!" he croaked, tugging at his collar.

"That doesn't seem like very much time."

"Poppycock, Mr. Asquith! You could deliver the confession in under a minute and work out a couple of simple plans in a half hour of sincere cogitation. Two days is pure luxury."

He looked about as excited as a man on the gallows who was being given an opportunity to avoid hanging by jumping off a tall building. Finally he said, "Very well. I'll do it."

"Very wise, sir. Please ask your wife to pop by on Monday so that we can conclude our business."

He lumbered to his feet and headed for the door.

When I returned to my flat I sent off a note to Mrs. Asquith telling her I had news about her husband and asking her to meet with me on Monday upon my return from the countryside. My hope was that Mr. Asquith would square things up with her by then, sparing me the never-pleasant task of reciting the tawdry details of a husband's secret life.

As I was on the front steps seeing off the courier another delivery boy dashed up with a telegram. I gave him a generous tip and asked him to wait while I read the telegram. It was from Sherlock, sent from Bavaria:

TRACKING OUR YOUNG ART STUDENT, HITLER. QUITE MAD BUT HAS A GROWING FOLLOWING HERE. HOPE TO RETURN TO LONDON NEXT WEEK. ECKART LIKELY STILL IN LONDON. MY RESEARCHES HERE INDICATE HE IS MORE

DANGEROUS THAN WE IMAGINED. TAKE PRECAUTIONS EVERYWHERE.

HOLMES

I scribbled out a reply, letting Sherlock know that I had Eckart under observation and was planning to see him shortly. I gave it to the delivery boy and sent him back to the telegraph office.

It was a fine day, sunny with wisps of high clouds, so after I packed my little overnight bag I hiked off to the station on foot. I wanted to get some blood moving in my body before I sat for three hours on the train to the Midlands. When I got to the station I bought a few items to snack on during the journey: a chunk of Caerphilly cheddar, a pack of Carr's Crackers and a generous piece of gingerbread sold to me by a lass who said she had baked it herself that morning.

I settled in for the journey and procured a glass of wine in the bar carriage, there to eat my snack. The rocking of the carriage along the tracks soon lulled me into slumber. When I awoke I barely had time to visit the loo and give my hair a pat down before we rumbled into Burley.

By the grace of our Benevolent Creator I had been to the Midlands on very few occasions, and then only to pass through on my way to Scotland. As every English traveler knows, the further you go north from London the less attractive the citizenry gets until you finally reach Edinburgh. Then and only then can you relax the squint in your eye. However, this was Burley, far short of Edinburgh, and I found I had to keep my gaze averted to keep my eyes from lingering too long on the odd shapes and rude apparel of the Midland folk.

When I got to my hotel I left my bag in the room and set off to have a bit of a look around the neighborhood. It wasn't hard to spot the mansion that Darcy's political sleepover was scheduled to take place in. It was called Burley-on-the-Hill, and there it was, up on the hill above town. The question that came automatically to mind was, "Why on earth would someone want to build a mansion in Burley?" I suppose its original owner must have been some reason he wanted to tower over Burley, but I was unable to fathom what it might be. I picture the tycoon who built it saying to his wife, "Dear, we have finally arrived—we tower over Burley!" Her breath catches and she pulls him toward the bedroom, "Quick, Nehemiah, I shall now perform the act you've been begging me for lo these forty years."

I still had a few hours to occupy before going up to the mansion for dinner, so I decided to hike up the hill and have a gander at it in daylight. A brochure I picked up at the hotel boasted about the architecture of the house, supposedly designed by none other than Sir Christopher Wren himself, greatest of all English architects.

When I got up to the mansion I found it a bit of a disappointment. It was a typical brick monstrosity, a block of three stories flanked by one-story wings that jutted off its eastern and western end. The striking feature of the place was its windows, several dozen of them all laid out in perfect symmetry across the front of the house. Up close it looked more like a hotel than a grand house.

I strolled around the grounds for a bit and then headed back down the hill to have a lie-down before dinner. When I unlocked my room, though, I discovered something that gave me a jolt of alarm: someone had searched my overnight bag while I was gone.

Before I left for my walk I had opened the bag to get out my leather toiletries kit, so I could give my teeth a quick brush before I set out. I had left the bag open on my bed, with the intention of unpacking it when I returned. I glanced in the bathroom and saw the kit was still there, but the space it had occupied in my bag was now gone. I was in the habit of packing my kit in the lower left hand corner of the bag; now my neatly folded sweater had been moved slightly so it occupied that spot. I felt the little hairs on the back of my neck stand to full attention.

I inspected the contents of the bag but couldn't see that anything was missing. I went in the bathroom and gave the kit a quick look-through. Nothing was missing there, either. If my visitor were an ordinary thief, he must not have found anything worth stealing.

However, I had a suspicion that my visitor had been combing through my meager belongings for some other purpose. I didn't know if it was my mind playing a trick on me, but when I opened the door to my room I could have sworn I caught a whiff of that odd, metallic scent I'd sniffed in the ballroom where Eckart had been standing.

I pondered this unexpected turn of events while I bathed and shaved, but I was none the wiser when I finished dressing and set off on my evening. My legs were a bit creaky from my earlier hike, so I elected to take a carriage up the hill. Darkness was falling fast, accompanied by a chilly wind that was coming in gusts off the moor. The wind whipping back and forth made me glad I'd remembered to pack my cashmere scarf, now wrapped snugly around my neck.

We clop-clopped our way up the road to the mansion, but when we pulled into the driveway we saw a footman running toward us and waving his arms frantically. I leaned out the window to see what the fuss was all about and smelled it at the same time I saw it: Smoke was pouring out of the windows of one of the side wings of the mansion.

"Pull out of the way!" the footman yelled, waving us over to the side of the driveway. "They've gone to fetch the fire wagon!"

I got out of the carriage and paid off the driver. "You can go. I'll find another way down later." The grateful cabbie tipped his hat to me and left at a trot back down the road.

I jogged off toward the fire to see if I could lend a hand. A dozen or so young men and women were gathered outside, all dressed in formal clothes. On the other side near the kitchen another group was clinging together, mostly women in aprons.

I asked one of the young men what happened.

"A fire broke out in the kitchen and spread into the dining room. Fortunately we were in the drawing room assembling for drinks."

"Is everyone evacuated?"

"All but one of us. He has foolishly gone back in to rescue a work of art."

Suddenly a young fellow burst out of a smoking door with a marble bust clutched in one arm and some manuscripts in the other. He set the objects down on the grass and stood beside them panting. As his colleagues rushed to his side I realized that the hero was none other than the wayward boyfriend of young Clemmie, with whom I'd shared the awkward dance at the last political gathering.

"Let us give thanks no one was injured," the young man cried out. The assembled crowd applauded and shouted BRAVO!

I heard bells clanging behind me and turned to see the fire wagon come charging up, a team of sturdy men clinging to it and drawn by four horses at full gallop. They pulled the wagon up close to the burning building and set about putting out the fire.

Looking at the chaos and the hoard of people milling around, it appeared that I might need to make other dinner plans. I had come specifically to have a close-up look at Dietrich Eckart, but as I scanned the crowd I failed to see him anywhere. Neither could I see any taxi to take me back down the hill. Rather than wait for things to sort themselves out, I decided to walk back down to the village and have myself a proper dinner.

I set off down the hill in the darkness, with nary a sliver of moon to light my way. I was only a few hundred yards down the road when I caught the scent of rain on the wind. I was not armed with my bumbershoot, not having planned to spend any time outdoors. Sure enough, the next gust brought a prickle of tiny raindrops to my face, and within a few minutes a chilly drizzle was settling in on my noggin. For vanity's sake I had gone out into the evening without a hat, opting to forgo a warm head so not to risk mussing the contours of my pompadour. Now, my carefully constructed locks had deflated completely, with dewlaps of wet hair hanging down around my ears. I feared I would arrive at the hotel looking like a bedraggled Airedale back from a long night on the stray.

My ears pricked up at the clop-clop sound of an approaching carriage, coming from the direction of the fire. I turned around and saw the lantern on a carriage bobbing along as a one-horse conveyance came slowly down the hill. The driver said, "Evening, sir," and pulled to a halt next to me.

The passenger door opened and I was surprised to see a bald-headed gentleman of my acquaintance. It was none other than the man himself, Dietrich Eckart, who gave me a formal bow and said, "May I offer you a ride, Sir Errol?"

I stood in the rain momentarily befuddled. If Dietrich Eckart were indeed the devil, it couldn't be a good thing to accept a ride from him. In fact, I distinctly remember Grandmother Hyde giving me stern warnings against "riding with the Devil." However, to my saintly grandmother's great chagrin, I had never put much stock in all that heaven and hell nonsense.

Besides, one should never let one's prejudices get in the way of a good adventure, so I gave him a hearty "Thank you, Herr Eckart!" and climbed aboard.

He said, "A night full of surprises, is it not?"

His English was very precise and almost accent-free, save for a tendency to add a slight hiss to his s's.

"Indeed. However, it has turned out most auspiciously in one way. I had hoped to get to know you better, and lo and behold, fate brings us together in a carriage."

"We should drink to that," he said. He reached into his coat and extracted a burnished silver pocket flask.

I started to demur but got swayed by three magic words.

He said, "I have an excellent little cognac with me—the Pierre Ferrand *Ancestrale*."

That got my attention. "My word! I've only tasted the *Ancestrale* once and it was transcendental." At my local spirits emporium it went for more than one hundred pounds a bottle, making it almost literally worth its weight in gold.

He said, "I think you'll find this vintage especially spiritual in its qualities."

He offered me the flask to taste the first sip. I was relieved, as I tend to be somewhat picky about where I put my mouth, concerned as any thoughtful person should be with the transmission of disease by oral means. The bumptious Dr. Jung had even gone so far as to refer to me as "germ-phobic," simply because I admitted to giving my hands a thorough scrub at least ten times during the course of a day.

I swirled the golden elixir around in my mouth and let it slide down my throat. It was rich, gorgeous and intriguing, with a round bottom of honeyed caramel and a lilting hint of floral perfume in the nose.

"Judging from the expression on your face, Sir Errol, I believe you find the beverage pleasing."

"Stunning," I said. I felt the spirit course its way down to my stomach, spreading out into a bloom of warmth that suffused my middle.

Eckart poured a tot of cognac into the cap of the flask and quaffed it off in one swallow. I was glad to see his lips hadn't touched the flask, as I was quite certain I was going to want more. As if reading my mind, he passed the flask back over to me and said, "I've found that the true essence of a great cognac is not revealed until the second or third sip. Please enjoy a bit more."

He had no trouble convincing me to take a second sip, then a third. As we clopped along the road, the inside of my body began to take on a golden glow. Before going up to the party I had fortified myself with a few puffs of the grey Lebanese hashish I employ to amplify my affability in social situations. I could still feel its benign buzz in my body, and this, combined with the golden glow of the cognac, was filling me with an absolute conviction that all was right with the world.

Eckart leaned forward and said, "Although our ride to the hotel will be brief, perhaps we can fill our time with something other than small-talk."

"Fine with me," I said. "Big Talk is always preferable to small-talk."

He chuckled at my witticism. "Then tell me a bit about yourself, Sir Errol. You are well known in certain circles for the brilliance of your abilities as a detective. To what do you attribute the skills for which you are so justly recognized?"

"Many people have asked me that, Herr Eckart, and to satisfy the public's curiosity I plan to write a book someday to explain my central method."

"And what will you call this book?"

"I've already got the title picked out. It's called *The Art Of Detection By Bumbling About*."

"Bumbling about! Is that is the main principle the brilliance of your detecting is based on?"

"Indeed. Nothing is so effective as simply bumbling about with curious intent."

"With respect, I'm not sure that title will help your reputation or your book sales."

"That's why I plan to write it much later in my career. For now I am working on a book that has pictures in it."

"I'm sure that will do better. Pictures have so much more appeal to people in these hurried times."

"Quite so. In fact, I'm surprised someone hasn't invented a way to beam pictures into people's homes, so they wouldn't have to put up with the ruckus of these new public houses that show moving pictures on the walls."

"Not to worry. Colleagues of mine are working on it. And when that invention comes into being we will be able to impose a great deal more order on humanity."

Up close to him, I could see the gleam of the fanatic in his eyes. It inspired me to goad him a bit.

"Order, eh? I think it would have the exact opposite effect. It would make it possible to broadcast every sort of craziness right into people's homes. Chaos would ensue."

"Yes, of course, unless one had control of what was broadcast into their homes."

"And how would one do that?"

He took off his glasses and began polishing them furiously with a spotless handkerchief. Without his glasses, I could see that his eyes were red-rimmed and twitching from side to side.

"We must unite behind a strong man, one who is willing to see the job through to its completion."

"What would that completion look like?"

"The undesirable elements will be gone, all the gypsies and Jews and homosexuals and women cavorting about nude in the cabarets. We would purify and start anew."

"And these undesirables of which you speak: would they be asked politely to eliminate themselves, or would you propose to do it for them?"

He drew his mouth into a tight little circle of disapproval. "Is all of this a joke to you, Sir Errol?"

"I fear so. As the Hungarians say, 'Life is hopeless but not serious.' "

He shook his head impatiently.

I couldn't resist saying, "By the way, are Hungarians on your list for extermination?"

He snorted and said, "Enough of this! Let us get to the point, shall we, Sir Errol?"

"Beg pardon?"

"You have appeared in my life three times now. That stretches the boundaries of coincidence past the breaking point. Pray tell me—just what are you up to?"

"I ask the same of you, Herr Eckart. Just what are YOU up to?"

He drew himself up majestically and said, "I am saving the world from itself, Sir Errol. My colleagues and I intend to preserve the best of humanity and send our species into the future purified and thriving."

"And to do this you need to get rid of all the gypsies and Jews and cabaret dancers?"

"You are mocking me, Sir Errol."

"Guilty as charged, but someone should have stepped in and done it long before now."

"There you go again, turning everything into a witticism. You think your fabled British sense of humor will save humanity?"

"You think you will save humanity without it? Without a sense of humor there would be no humanity to preserve."

"Nonsense," he said. He turned in the seat and rapped sharply on the wall behind him. A moment later the carriage rolled to a stop. The door opened and the cabbie, a huge burly fellow, stuck his head in.

"Yes, Mr. Eckart?"

"Could you assist me for a moment, Bruno?"

"Certainly, sir." He pushed his bulk through the door, causing me to have to move over to accommodate him.

I put a bit of heat in my voice and said, "Eckart, just what is going on here?"

"You are becoming tedious, Sir Errol. Whatever your game is, I have grown tired of it. Please restrain him, Bruno."

Before I could react, the cabbie threw his massive arms around me and squeezed me so hard I could scarcely breathe. He hefted his body over against my legs and trapped them against the side of the carriage. I tried to get free of his grasp but could not do anything but squirm helplessly.

Eckart leaned forward and pushed up the sleeve of my jacket, exposing my forearm. He opened a little kit and took out a syringe. Every cell in my body suddenly wanted to get away but I couldn't get even get my feet to kick.

"Hold still," he said. "I don't wish to hurt you."

I got my teeth unclenched enough to say, "You have an odd way of showing it."

"Ah, yes, the famous Sir Errol wit. Let's see how long that lasts."

He found a place on my arm and tapped it a few times. "This will sting a little," he said.

The last thing I saw before everything faded to black was the cruel little smile playing around his mouth.

CHAPTER FIFTEEN

I woke up with a dull headache and a raging thirst. I looked around. Where was I?

I lay on my back on a sofa in a living room that looked vaguely familiar. I could not get my mind into focus enough to remember why I recognized my surroundings. I tried to sit up and realized my ankles were bound together.

A voice behind me called out, "He's awake."

I craned my neck around and saw Eckart's man, Bruno, standing in the kitchen doorway. It was then that I became aware of where I was: the cottage in Blenheim where I met Malcolm Stewart, Freda and Madame C.

Bruno came over and stared down at me. "You look terrible," he said.

"I'm not surprised, given that I have been drugged and lugged out here against my will."

"Take that up with the boss," he said.

"Very well, but I could do with a tall glass of water right about now."

He lumbered off to the kitchen and came back with my water, which I drank down in one long gulp.

Eckart strolled into my field of vision, wearing an apron and carrying a bowl of salad greens. He placed the bowl on the table and said, "I am making *spaetzle*, Sir Errol, a type of dumpling that's a specialty of mine. Would you care to partake?"

The sight of Eckart wearing an apron was almost too much to comprehend. Whatever it did to my mind, though, it snapped me even more fully awake.

"I'd be delighted," I said, "and if at all possible, could we dine without my legs bound together? I find that being forcibly restrained hampers my digestion."

He chuckled. "Of course. Bruno, please untie Sir Errol. Once he tastes my *spaetzle* he won't want to go anywhere, anyway."

My brain's wonder machinery began to fire on all cylinders. How did I end up in the cottage, anyway? And was there a connection between Eckart and Malcolm Stewart's crew?

I decided to ask instead of wonder. "How did you come to bring me here, Herr Eckart? Do you know Malcolm Stewart and Madame Cynthia?"

He laughed. "You told me all about the cottage while you were blissfully unconscious, Sir Errol. You even gave us directions on how to find it and on the way regaled us with tales of the exotic Madame C. Sodium pentothal in the right dose turns you into quite an affable babbler, Sir Errol, although your enunciation does tend to suffer a bit."

"I'm quite well aware of the effects of sodium pentothal, Herr Eckart. Tell me—did I reveal any other secrets you found amusing?"

The corners of his lips twitched. "You went on quite a rant about Lady Forsythia. You were irritated that she held secret for so long that she was roaming the groves of Lesbos."

They don't call sodium pentothal "truth serum" for nothing. I must have buried a batch of anger at Lady Forsythia. I suppose I felt so much relief after her confession that I failed to acknowledge my anger. I was still mad about being lied to for so long. Many people prefer the comforts of easeful ignorance to the rollercoaster ride of reality as it is. I am not one of those people. Give me the rollercoaster any day.

"Your Madame C appears to be quite a remarkable seer. You seemed awestruck that she had correctly predicted events that had not yet occurred."

"I take it, then, that you are not acquainted with Madame C?"

"No, but I certainly intend to be. I am in the process of having her and her companions detained in Europe, so that we may become better acquainted upon my return. I sent word to my people earlier today, and I have no doubt they will be captured quickly."

"Now that you know all my secrets, Herr Eckart, how about telling me some of yours?"

He gave me a bitter little smile. "Have you heard the old saying, that if you want something done correctly you must do it yourself?"

"Yes, I've heard that but found it remarkably unhelpful. I'm wretchedly incompetent at a great many things—if I want my plumbing or my cooking done well I must avoid at all costs doing it myself."

"There's the Sir Errol wit again. I'm sorry that you cannot seem to take anything seriously."

"I am equally sorry that your sense of humor is so seriously compromised."

He waved his hand dismissively. "Enough. You asked me to reveal my secrets, and my great secret is that I have no secrets. If you had the wit to read German newspapers you would see that my intentions and activities are covered most thoroughly."

"Very well, but since I am a hopeless dullard in the face of your radiant wit, perhaps you could give me a few headlines."

"It is quite simple. A new world order is required, and I am devoting all my time to mustering the consensus and will to put it into place."

"This new world order—is that the one where Jews and naked women aren't allowed?"

He sighed. "You would do well to simply listen for once, Sir Errol. You might actually learn something."

"You would do well to listen to yourself, Herr Eckart. You sound like every other crackpot who decided he was going to change the world. Haven't you noticed? They always make the world worse."

His face turned crimson red. "Not this time!"

"Why is that? Why should you succeed when it's always proved to be such obvious folly?"

"Because we now have a leader who can unite us—a man who is not afraid to take us all the way."

"Oh, really! And who is this great leader?"

"You met him at Mr. Poindexter's ill-fated party."

"I did?"

"Yes. Young Hitler."

"Are you serious? That over-heated little rodent?"

"Careful, Sir Errol. You are treading on dangerous ground."

"What about the other young fellow you brought to the party, the sickly-looking chess wizard? Is he going to be a great political leader, too?"

"Of course not. He just happens to be the best young chess player on the Continent. I am passionately devoted to the game, so when I travel I often bring along a worthy opponent to play against me whenever I get the urge for a match. That young man defeats me constantly, but I am learning all his tricks and it won't be long before I find a way to best him. Do you play, Sir Errol?"

"No. Board games and cards bore me to tears."

"Pity. Chess is especially useful for organizing the mind."

"Another argument against it. Better to simply sit back and enjoy the richness of the mind's frolics."

He regarded me with disapproval and gave his head a shake. "How I wish I could get you to understand my point of view, Sir Errol. You are such an intelligent person."

"I understand your point of view all too well, Herr Eckart, but I cannot embrace it for the reason you mention: I'm an intelligent person."

He sighed and called to Bruno. "You may serve our dinner now." He removed his apron and sat down at the table.

Although Eckart was loathsome in most every other respect, in the domain of *spaetzle* and wild mushroom sauce he was an absolute genius. I took my first bite and couldn't help exclaiming, "My goodness, Herr Eckart—this sauce is superb!" The soft, golden mounds of *spaetzle* were drenched in a creamy, earthy sauce that tasted of the forest's very essence. Until I took that first bite I hadn't realized how famished I was.

"Why thank you, Sir Errol. It is not easy to find morels mushrooms this time of year. Bruno had to scour the food hall at Harrod's to procure a sufficiency to make the sauce."

"Well worth the effort! I cannot salute your politics, Herr Eckart, but I am a convert to the noble cause of *spaetzle*!"

"I am glad your taste buds are able to transcend the differences between us. Now, let me tempt you with one more of my obsessions, Sir Errol. If my researches are correct, you are a man who enjoys a good cup of coffee. One of my informants tells me you drink the traditional English tea only as a beverage of last resort. Am I correct?"

I was intrigued, so I decided to set aside the question of just who these informants were. "You are quite correct. I find strong tea galling, and in this country they don't serve tea until it's so strong a spoon will stand up unassisted in the cup. A good cup of coffee, however, has a type of bitterness I find most agreeable, especially when graced by a dash of Devonshire cream."

His head bobbed with enthusiasm. "Then I think you are going to remember this moment all your life. Let me show you a machine that made its debut just two years ago at the Milan World's Fair. I believe it will revolutionize the coffee industry."

He led me into the kitchen and made a deep bow as he gestured toward a gleaming metal contraption on the stove. "I present to you the *La Pavoni* espresso machine, a device I now consider so indispensable to my lifestyle that I take it with me at some inconvenience wherever I go."

It was dome-shaped machine almost a yard high, with various pipes sticking out of it. Bruno handed Eckart a container of freshly ground coffee beans, which Eckart proceeded to pack into two metal cylinders attached to handles. He locked the cylinders into the machine and placed a cup underneath each cylinder. He gave me a wink and said, "Now watch this!"

He turned a knob and the machine began to hiss and clank. In a moment a rich black syrup of coffee began to stream into the cup, followed at the end by a mighty hissing of the machine and a thick layer of coffee foam. He handed a cup to me and said, "If I may suggest, please try one first without the addition of cream."

I took a sip and my world changed. Here was the very essence of coffee expressed in liquid and air. It was truly revolutionary—the inventor of the machine had harnessed the power of steam to release the full potential of the sacred bean! I was impressed.

"Sign me up," I said. "I need one of these in my kitchen as soon as humanly possible."

He chuckled. "I had a feeling you would like it, Sir Errol, but I must give you a warning—the machine is more temperamental than an Italian soprano."

"I'll take my chances," I said.

"That's the spirit, my good fellow. But now that we have finished our pleasantries, we must return to the business at hand ... even if it is not so pleasant."

"Yes, let's not forget that your dinner invitation came via an injection of sodium pentothal."

"For that I must apologize, Sir Errol, but I could not risk your meddling in my activities. The stakes are too great."

"Earlier you said if you wanted something done correctly you must do it yourself. What is the exact task that you must do yourself?"

"I don't suppose there's any harm in telling you. There is a young gentleman who must be eliminated, a potential deterrent to the fulfillment of our plan. It is important to remove him from the chessboard, and I have taken personal responsibility for doing so. I entrusted others to do it for me on two separate occasions, both of which resulted in failure. So now I come to take care of it myself."

"And this fellow is here in Blenheim?"

"Not quite yet. My informants tell me he will be here at the estate later today to meet a young lady to whom he intends to propose. Perhaps if we can catch them together we can kill two birds with one stone."

"Somehow I am getting the impression you are not the most romantic of men, Herr Eckart. The young lady has done nothing to impede your so-called plan. Why kill an innocent person?"

"Why would she want to live if her fiancé is dead? We might as well put her out of her misery."

"Has it not occurred to you that women have a value beyond being marriage fodder?"

"You chide me for not being romantically inclined, Sir Errol, but aren't you perhaps being overly romantic in your assessment of women? I know there is much agitation these days of women getting to vote, attend universities and the like, but I assure you it is just a passing fancy. Once women have seen how corrupt the man's world really is, they will stampede back to the kitchen and bedroom. Women have served quite well for thousands of years as breeding stock; let us not ask more of them."

"I find your opinions quite repellent, Herr Eckart."

"Just as repellent as I find your misguided liberalism, Sir Errol. Now, I must leave to carry out my little task. This will likely be the last time we see each other, so let me bid you a fond farewell."

"So, I take it you do not need to remove me permanently from the chessboard?"

He laughed. "Heavens, no. I need you to help spread the word! We will give you another injection to keep you quiet and you will wake up in a few hours to a different world. You will simply need to find your own ride back into London, which I'm sure a clever detective such as yourself will be able to do."

"What about my Derringer? I noted that it is missing from my pocket."

"We'll stick it back in your pocket after you're asleep. By the way, that pistol of yours is a joke, as I'm sure you know. If your target stands more than a few paces away, you would likely do more damage by hurling a rock at him. I'm surprised: why doesn't Sir Errol Hyde, the great detective, carry a more substantial weapon?"

"In England, Herr Eckart, a gentleman does not ridicule the size of another man's weapon. However, to answer your question, I find that larger pistols cause an unsightly bulge in my jacket."

"Ah, yes—vanity... always the vanity with Sir Errol! Bruno, fetch his ridiculous little pistol. And bring me the syringe."

He gestured to the sofa. "Please sit back down."

Bruno's massive bulk hovered over me, so there was nothing I could do but go along with him. I sank back and awaited my fate.

He pinched up a piece of skin on my arm and stuck the needle in. "So long, Sir Errol. Pleasant dreams." He withdrew the syringe and handed it to Bruno, and as my head was getting foggy I saw them heading off toward the kitchen. An idea suddenly flashed through my darkening mind—I pinched the skin around the injection site and brought it to my mouth, sucking hard until I could taste blood. I spat it out and pinched the area harder, sucking for all I was worth until I could get no more blood. Then darkness overtook me and I sank into the void, the taste of my own blood on my tongue.

. . .

It must have worked, because when I woke up I looked at the clock and saw that less than an hour had gone by. When I stood up my head felt a little woozy, but other than that my body appeared to work reasonably well. I walked around the place getting my feet steady on the ground, and then propelled by hope, peered into the kitchen to see if perhaps by chance Eckart had forgotten to take his espresso machine. Another cup of that excellent brew would clear my head marvelously. No such luck. The machine was gone. I glanced around the rest of the house; with the exception of the crumpled napkins and a few crumbs on the table there was no sign anyone had ever been there.

I paused to assess my situation. On my previous trip I'd gotten a cursory look at Blenheim Palace. The territory covered by the great house, its outbuildings and grounds was vast. Where would I even begin to look?

Suddenly I remembered the bright young girl I'd encountered on my earlier trip. I wracked my fuzzy brain for her name and finally remembered that she was "Freddy," short for Fredericka. Perhaps she or her father could help me get the lay of the land.

I dashed out of the cottage and jogged off down the trail through the woods where I'd last seen Freddy and her dog. In a hundred yards I came out into a clearing and saw a modest stone cottage with smoke coming out of the chimney. I ran up and knocked on the door. In a moment the door flew open and Freddy greeted me with a happy exclamation. "Sir Errol!"

"Hallo, Freddy!"

She called over her shoulder, "Da, it's the gentleman I told you about."

Her father came limping to the door. He was a big fellow with a weathered, kind face and an iron gray beard. I shook his rough hand. "Hello, sir. I'm Errol Hyde."

"A pleasure, Sir Errol. I'm John Penn. Freddy told me all about meeting you. Would you like to come in?"

I had to duck slightly to get through the door. Their living room was modestly furnished—a wooden table and a few handmade chairs—but it was spotlessly clean and tidy. Freddy's flop-eared hound was stretched out by the fireplace and snoring lustily. I noticed cups and a teapot on the table.

"I hope I didn't interrupt your tea, but I'm in a bit of a hurry."

"It's all right—how can we help?"

"I have reason to believe a crime is going to take place at the palace today, a crime I must at all costs prevent."

"What sort of crime?"

"I fear the worst sort of crime."

"Good God! Who is the intended victim?"

"I don't know. All I know is that it is a young man who will be proposing to a young woman today."

Freddy said, "Lady Jenny's son?"

"I don't know. Why do you ask that?"

"I've never met him but she told me her son has been, in her words, "dithering about" with one woman and another. She wishes him to pick one and settle down."

Freddy's father said, "The estate is large. Do you have any idea where it might take place?"

"I do!" Freddy cried, surprising her father and myself.

"Where?"

"The Temple Of Diana, Da! It's the obvious place!"

I asked them what it was.

"It's a little ornamental Greek temple down by the lake. There's a summerhouse with beautiful gardens around it."

Her father said, "Freddy could be right! It's the most romantic place on the grounds."

It sounded like a good possibility. "How far is it?"

"Twenty minutes for you to walk it." He pointed down at his foot, which I hadn't noticed was wrapped in bandages. "I'm afraid I'm not going to be of much help to you. I took a fall the other day."

Freddy piped up, "I have a better idea!"

"Yes?"

She pointed to her hound still sound asleep by the fireplace. "Humphrey's nose is ever so keen. Do you have anything with the scent of your man on it? Humphrey could take us right to him."

A picture of crumpled napkins flickered through my mind. "I might. I'll dash back and get it while you attempt to awaken our Humphrey from his slumbers."

I jogged back through the woods to the cottage and picked up the napkin I'd seen Eckart toss on the table. When I got back to Freddy's cottage I found Humphrey wagging his tail enthusiastically at the front door.

"Let him sniff your hand first," Freddy said.

I presented my hand to Humphrey and he gave it a thorough sniffing.

"Now he knows what you smell like, let him sniff the handkerchief. He'll be able to tell you from the other man who touched it."

I held out the handkerchief for Humphrey to smell, which he did with a great deal of snuffling and snorting.

"Now let's take him back over to the cottage and see if he can pick up the trail. Don't worry, Da, I'll stay out of trouble."

Her father was obviously a wise man. He didn't try to argue with her; instead he cautioned me by saying, "Please be careful. She's all I've got."

I felt a shiver in my spine as I accepted the responsibility. "I give you my solemn word. I will allow no harm to come to Freddy."

We left in haste and ran through the woods to the cottage, with Humphrey trotting along on his stubby legs beside us. When we got to the cottage I gave him another sniff of the handkerchief. Freddy pointed to the ground and he put his nose down to it and barked. He jogged off in front of us down the road and we ran to keep up. When he got to a fork in the road he dashed up one, then the other, before taking off down the road to the left.

We hustled along behind him on a little dirt road that skirted the backside of the estate.

Freddy pointed to a distant structure, shrouded in swirls of mist. "He's taking us right toward the Temple Of Diana."

As we legged along behind Humphrey I felt a few splats of raindrops on my head and instantly regretted not bringing a hat or an umbrella. Freddy was bundled in a thick wool sweater and I had on my travel jacket, so I wasn't worried about us getting a chill in the rain. I just have trouble thinking straight when my head is wet. I use a modest dollop of pomade on my locks, and if my hair gets wet it drips down my face in an unpleasant manner.

Humphrey wriggled his chunky body under a wooden fence and set off across open land. By the time we clambered over the fence we could hear him barking in the distance. We ran toward his barking and saw Eckart's carriage parked next to a clump of trees. Humphrey was barking at the door of the carriage, which from a distance looked empty. I felt for the Derringer in my jacket pocket.

Suddenly I saw Bruno with his back to us behind the carriage and realized we had caught him in the act of urinating. He spun around, buttoning up his trousers, and caught sight of us running toward him. He dashed to the front of the carriage and grabbed a long-barreled revolver off the seat.

Freddy yelled, "Humphrey! Bad man!" and pointed to Bruno.

Humphrey bolted to Bruno and began biting at his ankles. Bruno bellowed and took a swipe at Humphrey with the barrel of his pistol, whacking Humphrey's head with it. Humphrey yelped and backed up, snarling and jumping around.

Bruno aimed the pistol at Humphrey and that's when I jerked up my arm and fired the Derringer.

Bruno let out a roar and stumbled backward, clutching his shoulder and dropping the gun on the ground. He stooped over to pick it up with his other hand, but Humphrey chose that moment to mount another attack. He bounded forward and snapped at Bruno's hand, preventing Bruno from picking up the gun. Then he went for Bruno's ankle again and landed a bite. Bruno kicked at Humphrey, then turned around and sprinted for the cover of the forest. Humphrey took off in hot pursuit but Freddy let out a piercing whistle and yelled, "Humphrey, stop!"

The hound screeched to a halt and looked back at Freddy. The poor fellow appeared a bit crestfallen; he probably thought he had done something wrong. Freddy ran to his side and dropped down on her knees, giving him a hug and a pet. Fortunately Humphrey was blessed with a short attention span and a disinclination to hold a grudge. He put on a doggy-grin and began wagging his stubby tail furiously.

Freddy let him sniff the handkerchief again, reminding him of our true quarry. He sat bolt upright and then chugged off as fast as his little legs could carry him toward The Temple Of Diana. I picked up Bruno's heavy revolver and set off after Freddy and the dog.

Crack!

The sky lit up with a flash of lightning as a boom of thunder rolled echoing across the moors. Seconds later there was another thunderclap and we were suddenly pelted by rain. I quickened my pace to keep up with Freddy who was dashing after Humphrey. I caught up with them and realized that the dog was frozen in his tracks, shivering.

Freddy knelt to his side and clutched his quaking body to her. "He doesn't like thunder," she said.

I could see The Temple Of Diana straight ahead about a quarter-mile in the mist. I said, "Stay here and look after Humphrey. I'm going on ahead. Please keep a safe distance."

She nodded. "I'm going to take Humphrey over there under the trees." She picked up the poor fellow, still quivering with fear, and carried him off holding him like a baby in her arms.

I ran toward the temple covering my head with one hand and the revolver in the other. The revolver's foot-long barrel was far too large to stick in a pocket, so I was forced to lope along holding its five-pound heft in my hand. As I grew closer to the temple I could see a man and a woman taking shelter from the rain under its eves. They were holding hands.

My God! Madame C's vision was becoming reality before my very eyes. A flicker off to my left caught my attention. There was Eckart, moving stealthily toward the temple, his own revolver in his hand. He was so intent on his approach that he didn't appear to notice my own.

I slowed down my trot and veered over to the shelter of a tree about twenty yards behind Eckart. By now the rain was coming down hard, making a deafening roar that helped conceal my footsteps as I stole up behind Eckart.

When I was about ten feet behind him I said, "Please to halt," and pointed the gun at his back.

He spun around, raising his own pistol until he saw mine pointed at his chest. He slowly lowered the gun to his side. His wicked grin spread across his face.

"Sir Errol! What a surprise! Have you done something terrible to Bruno?"

"Never mind Bruno," I said. "Let that pistol drop to the ground."

He didn't drop the pistol. "I don't think so," he said. "I see your arm shaking with the weight of that pistol. Your body is telling you not to use it. Listen to your body, Sir Errol."

"My body is telling me to put a hole in your chest and put a stop to all your nonsense."

He laughed. "You think by shooting me you can stop our movement? That's ridiculous, Sir Errol—you cannot stop history."

"Oh, so history is on your side, is it?"

"Just wait and see. Your kind is on the way out."

"My kind, eh? What precisely is 'my kind'?"

"All your countrymen, with your famous English wit and your so-called democracy and your decadent forms of art. Your weak arms that cannot hold a pistol without shaking like a leaf."

He had me there. My arm was beginning to ache from holding the pistol in my out-stretched hand. I suddenly regretted that I seldom lifted anything heavier than a billiard cue or a golf club. I reached out with my left hand and shifted the pistol over into it.

Unfortunately it was the hand that had been covering my head; it was still slick with water and pomade. The pistol slipped from my grip and dropped on the ground.

I heard Eckart let out a sharp bark of laughter as the tables turned. His pistol was now aimed at my chest. Over his shoulder I saw the couple in the little Greek temple clasp each other in an embrace. The young man dropped to one knee before the young lady.

Eckart saw the direction of my gaze and canted his head around so he could see what I was looking at. "Ah, there's my chance," he said. He aimed the gun at me and I saw his finger tighten on the trigger. I spun to my left just as a bolt of lightning and a clap of thunder exploded. I saw the muzzle flash of his shot, the sound buried in the thunder. The bullet tore a hole in the sleeve of my jacket and I felt a flash of burning sensation on my elbow.

Eckart whipped the aim of his pistol back and forth between the temple and me. In his moment of indecision I launched myself at him in a flying rugby tackle, crashing my head into his middle. We went down in a heap, with him whacking at my head with his pistol. I got my hand on its long barrel and twisted with all my might. I heard the wet pop of his trigger finger dislocating as he let out a roar of rage and backed up clutching his hand. I could see the joint of his finger sticking out at a right angle as he winced from the pain.

I picked up my pistol and got it aimed at him again. He got his breathing under control and looked at me with hatred pouring out of his eyes.

"Now what will you do, Sir Errol? A proper English gentleman would never shoot a man in cold blood."

"I'm afraid you are right, Eckart. I cannot shoot you, nor do I have the means to detain you."

"Then let me go. I will catch the evening channel crossing and be in Calais by midnight. We will live to fight another day."

"Ah, the hypocrisy! You were just mocking our English ways, but here you are, begging to be the beneficiary of English mercy."

He shrugged. "Life is filled with such ironies. So how about it, Sir Errol?"

I gestured with the barrel of my pistol toward the woods. "If you make haste you may be able to catch up with Bruno."

He gave me a curt nod and ran off into the forest.

I tucked the guns under a bush and looked out to see what the young lovers were doing. The young man was just getting up off his knees and enveloping the young lady in a full embrace. I walked toward them, not knowing exactly why. The young man caught sight of me and pointed me out to his beloved, who turned in my direction.

As I reached the shelter of the temple I had a wave of vanity, regretting my torn sleeve and plastered-down hair.

"Sir Errol!" the young woman cried out. I realized it was young Clemmie, with whom I'd danced briefly at the political gathering.

Her young man stepped forward, inspecting me curiously. He stuck out his hand. "Hello, Sir Errol. I don't think I've had the pleasure. My name is Winston. Winston Churchill. Welcome to my family home."

"Pleased to meet you," I said. "I am Errol Hyde."

He gestured to Clemmie. "This is Lady Clementine Hozier, whom you already appear to have met. Clemmie just made me the happiest man in the world by accepting my proposal of marriage."

I gave them my heartfelt congratulations and good wishes for their union.

Clemmie said, "Sir Errol, I'm very curious. What brought you to Blenheim today?"

"I promise to tell you all about it later, my dear lady. It's quite a long story, but it has one or two features of interest." I gestured to the summerhouse behind the temple. "In the meantime, I wonder if there is a telephone inside that I might use."

CHAPTER SIXTEEN

After many clicks, clunks and delays I finally got through to Scotland Yard and heard the voice of Inspector Dinwoodie on the telephone. I explained the situation to him, giving him detailed descriptions of Eckart and Bruno. He agreed to apprehend the two at Dover or mount a search for them if they didn't appear at the channel crossing in the evening.

After I hung up I went outside to look for the happy couple. I found them back in the temple holding hands and deep in conversation. I bid them a fond farewell and promised to see them again back in London. Then I legged it back up the road in search of Freddy and Humphrey, discovering to my relief that they were both where I'd last seen them. I was also happy to find that my canine friend was now back in good fettle and standing on his sturdy little legs.

On our way back down the road I gave Freddy a sanitized version of the story, one I hoped would not alarm her father.

"Oh, look, they left it behind," she said, pointing to the clump of trees where Eckart's carriage was still parked.

A hopeful idea flickered through my mind. I jogged over to the carriage and took a look in the rear storage compartment. There it was, gleaming in all its glory, the espresso machine. I decided on the spot to award it to myself as a bonus for a job well done.

Freddy said, "Why don't we take the carriage back to my cottage? We can get Da to help us figure out what to do with it and the horse."

"Excellent idea," I said, "but with one small caveat. I have no idea how to drive a carriage."

"Sir Errol, you silly! It's a snap!" She jumped into the driver's seat and got Humphrey arranged between us. Then she did some kind of magical twitch with the reins that made the horse start forward. She steered us smartly all the way back to the cottage, where the door burst open and her father hobbled out looking relieved. Freddy jumped out, gave her Da a hug and began chattering about our adventure.

Later they took me in the carriage back to the station, where I caught a train and rode back into London accompanied by the espresso machine in the seat beside me.

When I got back to my flat I found a telegram waiting for me. It was from Sherlock Holmes:

RETURNING LONDON TOMORROW. MET MADAME C, STEWART AND FREDA, WILL RETURN TOGETHER. HOPE ECKART CAUSED YOU NO TROUBLE.

HOLMES

I scribbled a quick reply and called for a courier to take it to the telegraph office.

I wrote:

ECKART WAS NO TROUBLE AT ALL. PLEASE COME ROUND WHEN YOU RETURN AND ALL WILL BE EXPLAINED.

HYDE

As I was lugging the machine into my flat I saw Francesca coming up the stairs.

"Sir Errol! I've been worried about you! Is all well?"

"Beyond well, my dear Francesca. I virtually hum with anticipated bliss! You must come in and help me learn to operate this new machine."

She glanced at it and said, "Wonderful! Now we can have espresso!"

"You are familiar with these machines?"

"Of course I am. They were invented in the part of Italy where I'm grew up. Come, I'll show you how they work."

And so she did. We put the machine on the stove, and while the flame heated the water we set about grinding beans and tamping them into the little cylinder. When the steam was ready she locked the cylinder into place, put two small cups under the spout and turned the knob. The machine hissed and a thick stream of espresso began to chuckle into the cups. We clinked them together in toast and took our sips of the splendiferous liquid.

As I savored its rich flavor a question sprang to mind. "Since you are so kind as to make my coffee in the morning, shall we keep the machine down in your flat?"

"No, let's keep it up here," she said.

Suddenly it occurred to me that she might be about to inform me she was moving out to Bratty's mansion.

"My dear Francesca! Have you accepted a proposal from Mr. Poindexter?"

"No, no," she said, a shy smile playing about her lips. "It's just that ..." she paused and took a breath, "I hope soon to be spending more time up here."

My mind went blank: Whatever could she mean by that?

The End

(Answers to this and other mystifying conundrums will be revealed in *The Second Adventure of Sir Errol Hyde: The Case of The Oxford Rasputin*)

READ A SAMPLE FROM THE NEW BOOK!

THE SECOND ADVENTURE OF SIR ERROL HYDE

THE CASE OF THE OXFORD RASPUTIN

Gay Hendricks

Dear Readers,

First, let me offer you an extravagant bouquet of thanks for your warm-hearted reception of the first volume of my adventures. It was my first book, so I hope you will forgive me if I strut and crow for a moment. My publishers tell me they are thrilled with the sales so far. I have gently suggested on several occasions that the numbers could be improved if they put a bit more attention into publicity, but they just tell me to keep writing the books and let them worry about selling them.

I took time off for a spot of rest after my last adventure, dedicating myself to several months of sheer, naked pleasure—with special emphasis on the 'naked.' During part of my vacation I went for a stroll in the Lake District, a two-week sojourn intended to replace the London soot in my nostrils with something resembling fresh air.

I had the very highest intentions of keeping only my own company on the journey, so that I could best devote myself to the natural wonders of the fabled region. However, my compassionate nature got the better of me again, forcing me to abandon my solo occupations for the better part of a week so that I could properly console a widow.

This particular widow operated the bed and breakfast in Ambleside at which I arrived one night, desperate to get out of a pouring rain and so hungry that the smell of soup cooking in her kitchen nearly brought me to tears.

It turned out that I was her only guest, November being a somewhat dreary time of the year when few people are moved to tread the charming footpaths of the district. I was grateful to see the warm smile on her face, and doubly pleased to observe, as I let my eyes wander downward, that her attractive features included a lushly proportioned arrangement of bosom and hips. She introduced herself as

Mamie Ford and proceeded to express her gratitude for my arrival in ways that far exceeded the typical obligations of hospitality required of innkeepers.

She studied the look on my face and said, "You must be famished. Could I offer you a bowl of soup? It's a simple soup made from wild mushrooms I picked today, topped with a dollop of Devonshire cream."

It sounded delicious and anything but simple. In fact, it seemed like about the best idea I'd ever heard in my life. I gave her a grateful "Yes" and plunked myself down at the table. In a moment she brought out a steaming bowl of thick, brown soup crowned with a generous tot of clotted cream. She sprinkled a scoop of crisp, buttery croutons over the top and set the soup before me. I paused for a moment to savor the earthy aroma, then seized my spoon and dove in.

My chef and benefactor beamed at me with approval as I sipped and slurped my way through the soup. It tasted of the very essence of the deep forest; one spoonful of Mrs. Ford's fine soup and I was transported back to the hunter-gatherer era. It is a testament to the glories of her soup that it made me romanticize the cave-dweller lifestyle, given that I loathe camping with an intensity of passion I usually reserve for my dislike of okra, ballet and pub darts.

When not the tiniest bit of soup was left in the bowl I put down my spoon and sat back with a sigh of utter satisfaction. "That was brilliant," I said.

"I'm so glad you liked it. Would you care to finish with a spot of coffee or tea and a slice of banana cake I made this afternoon?"

"A cup of coffee would be most restorative, my dear lady. As for the cake, after tasting your soup I have taken a lifetime vow never to turn down any food you offer me."

"Why, thank you, Mr. Hyde. And if I may say, you certainly have a way with words!"

"So I'm told," I said, modestly of course.

Over coffee and her deliciously moist cake, Mrs. Ford and I fell into an unexpectedly deep conversation in which she told me the story of her husband's demise in a climbing accident. Later, when we had moved on the cognac phase of the evening, we sat before the fireplace and talked about the mysteries of relationships.

She revealed she had lived an exotic early life as a hostess in several London gaming clubs, before deciding on a whim to marry a hiking-guide and retire to the bucolic charms of the Lake District. In turn, I regaled her with some of my misadventures in the booby-trapped fields of love. She also surprised me with a confession about the death of her husband, that her brief marriage had been an awful struggle. She told me she still felt a sense of guilt, because along with the shock and sadness of her husband's death she had also felt a sense of deep relief.

Never one to let a woman suffer needlessly, I attempted to assuage her guilt a bit. "It is natural that you would feel guilty about your sense of relief, because nobody ever talks about that particular emotion. I've never once heard anybody at a funeral say, 'I am so very relieved that our friend is dead.' We prattle on about what a fine fellow he was or what a great saint she was, but few of us feel bold enough to speak up and say what everybody is secretly feeling: 'Let's all bow our heads and remember that sometimes our friend could be absolutely obnoxious.' "

My guilt-removal treatment appeared to be meeting with some success; I was pleased to see my utterances were getting a chuckle or two out of her.

I found myself wondering: Could this rather jolly widow, who had so warmed my belly with her magnificent soup, also be enticed to warm my bed this very night? I felt the hopeful stirrings of lust deep in the woolen reaches of my hiking trousers.

Such was my good fortune that I had sought lodging at the perfect place and time to serve a healing role in the life of this young widow. It had been a year since her husband's plunge off the mountain, and she had reached that time in her widowhood when a woman, particularly one who has been around the block a few times, suddenly decides she wants to go around a few more.

I had hoped that hiking in the Lake District would help me rid myself of a few unwanted pounds that had recently convened around my mid-section. However, my consolation of the widow proved to be so time-consuming that I hardly set foot upon the storied by-ways of the region. The week of horizontal cavorting in Mrs. Ford's bedroom was unable to offset the marvelous meals she cooked for us. I waddled out of the Lake District with all the extra heft I'd lugged in plus a few pounds more.

After saying many fond goodbyes, I left a happy widow behind and departed post-haste for a health spa down by the sea in Brighton. They fed me leafy greens, fresh fruits and brown rice for a week until I was lean as a whippet and ready again for the rigors of London social life.

When I returned, it didn't take long for a new adventure to come knocking at my door.

Now, dear Readers, I believe I've brought you up to date. If you are ready to embark with me on my second adventure, let us proceed without further preamble.

Your humble scribe,
Sir Errol Hyde

CHAPTER ONE

The morning after I returned to London, the lovely Francesca came up from the flat below, as usual, to make me a cup of her fine cappuccino. Readers of my last adventure may remember that I came away from that case with a splendid espresso machine, liberated from the clutches of the arch-miscreant, Dietrich Eckart. Francesca enjoyed a keen resonance with the machine, hailing as she did from the north of Italy where espresso was invented, and so had taken on its operation as her own special province.

After she brought our cups of coffee she settled beside me on the sofa. "I say, Sir Errol, when you've finished savoring your morning cup I was wondering if I could have a word."

Ah, I thought, the moment is upon us. Francesca had intoned mysteriously a while back that she hoped to be spending more time in my flat in the coming year. Just what she meant by that was unclear to me at the time, but instead of asking her to elaborate I left her utterance dangling in the air, preferring to wait until she brought it up in her own time.

"Of course, dear Francesca. What's on your mind this beautiful day?"

I could feel a sensation in my belly halfway between excitement and fear. I was afraid Francesca was about to announce that she would be leaving our comfortable arrangement to marry her fervent suitor, my old classmate from Cambridge, John "Bratty" Poindexter. The possibility also excited me, being a cheerleader for Francesca's full flowering, because Bratty's vast fortune would help Francesca realize her dream of going to medical school, a step to her ultimate goal of becoming a psychoanalyst. Women had a difficult time getting into medical schools; Bratty's money and connections would give her an incomparable advantage. Come to that, Bratty could afford to buy her an entire medical school.

I would miss her, though. Not only did she make a fine cup of coffee, she had a perpetually sunny attitude and could also be called upon for occasional late-night mercy visits, employing her gentle and exquisitely skilled hands to relieve me of the tensions of the day and ease my transition into slumber.

As it turned out, the story I had concocted in my mind—marriage and the like—was complete blather. She wanted to talk to me about something utterly different.

"I'm very grateful to you, Sir Errol, for letting me stay rent-free in lodgings the likes of which I could never have afforded on my own."

"The pleasure is mine, dear Francesca. As you no doubt know, I find your companionship most valuable."

"Yes, you have expressed your appreciation in many ways, for which I'm extremely grateful. Now, though, I have a request that may go outside the bounds of our relationship in its current form."

She had me intrigued. "How so?"

"I have decided not to accept Mr. Poindexter's proposal of marriage, and I have also decided not to pursue medical studies at present."

I don't mind saying I was a bit flabbergasted. "You've caught me by surprise, my dear. Very well, then, but what do you intend to do?"

She fixed her deep, green eyes on mine and said, "I want to be your apprentice. I want to learn the art of detection, on my way to becoming England's first female detective!"

I was stunned into silence for a moment. What an outrageously bold goal! I immediately warmed to it.

"My goodness, Francesca, this is wonderful news indeed! How did you come to such a conclusion?"

"It's very simple. I have been observing your activities all year long and, more recently, reading about the cases of Sherlock Holmes. I began to wonder: Why should the boys be having all the fun?"

Indeed.

And that is how Francesca Molinari became the first and only student of the Errol Hyde School Of Detection, studying the sacred art practiced by all master sleuths: bumbling about with curious intent.

Made in the USA
San Bernardino, CA
31 July 2017